Haunted by the Shadow of Death

LIFE AFTER DEATH DAY
BOOK 3

DONNA AUGUSTINE

Chapter One

IT FELT like centuries had passed since Death Day, when most of the world had died, and at least a decade since I'd left New York and come to Groza's pack with Duncan. It hadn't even been a month since I mated with Kicks and came here to the Arkansas pack's temporary compound. And yet here I was moving—*again*.

Kicks' pack bustled around the quaint street in front of the boutique hotel we'd been staying in. A dusting of snow covered the ground as the pack prepared to leave for Arkansas. A chilly wind blew, giving an excuse for the shiver that ran through me.

Kicks' pack didn't hold any of my fears and were near bristling with excitement about going home as they loaded up the ATVs and motorcycles as best they could. Any larger vehicle would be too difficult to navigate or gas-guzzling to manage. The highways and roads were a parade of crashes, a lasting calling card of Death Day that would remain until nature slowly covered the wreckages as the years passed. The bodies would slowly turn to dust, with too few of us left living to remember. Even fewer left after what had happened at Groza's pack.

My eyes were drawn north as I remembered what had happened there. If I squinted, I could see the top of the tallest building of the historic little village in the not-so-far-off distance. I'd thought I'd be living the rest of my life out there. I'd imagined raising Charlie there, with that pack. It hadn't been ideal, but nothing was since Death Day.

But the pack there had begun to accept us both—except for its alpha, Groza. If it hadn't been for her, I'd still be there in my little cabin. If she hadn't sent her thugs after me time and time again, maybe I wouldn't have so many deaths on my hands.

But she had, and I did.

Then I'd thought we'd be at this hotel for at least a few months. That Charlie would be able to see his friends for a while. Not now, not after what had happened. Not after the day when the pack had seen what I could truly do, killing with a touch. That reality had torn through any façade of cooperation between Kicks' pack and Groza's. According to the letter from Duncan, I'd be dead if I even set a foot back there.

So here we were, moving again. I was dragging my little brother Charlie to a new pack, a new home, a new set of unknowns. I'd be walking in blind, not knowing who was friend and who was foe. Once upon a time, I'd thought of moving like a fresh start. Now it felt like opening up another Pandora's box, waiting to see what would pop out next.

All the nasty surprises made me ache for the mundane. I wanted off this hamster wheel in hell. I didn't feel as if I were running on solid legs but bumping along the bottom, trying to find something to hold on to and everything breaking off in my grasp.

We still didn't know what had caused this utter upheaval in the world and caused so many to die in a single moment. Would we ever? How could we when no one had time to stop and take a breath, let alone investigate something of that scope? Life was a nonstop race to survive, and it might be like that until the day I died. One scramble after another, barely getting by before another disaster was lobbed at us.

My body suddenly seized. I could barely move in the middle of the hustling activity around me as I tried to breathe in air that felt too thin.

"Stop overthinking things," Widow Herbert said, cutting through the panic.

She was a ghost from my past that haunted my present, another life lost to the chaos. I'd never forget the day she died after crossing the river. I'd never stop regretting bringing her and feeling the weight of her death on my conscience.

"Are you paying attention to me?" she said, not one to be ignored. "You don't have time for an emotional crisis right now. These people around you, they are the ones who will be vouching for you at the new pack. You need to show strength. Fall apart when you're alone." Her gray hair was pulled back in a tight bun and her eyes saw too much.

For someone who used to be a psychologist, her advice sucked at the moment. Wasn't she supposed to help me talk through my feelings? What kind of crap was this? Swallow it down until no one could see and then collapse into a wreck all alone? Some therapy that was.

She must have read my thoughts, because she was rolling her eyes. "These aren't civilized times," she said, sounding more like a drill sergeant than someone concerned about my mental well-being. "A decade ago I would've let you come in and cry away on my couch, but that was before everything went to hell. Consider me more of a wartime consigliere, if you will. I'm more concerned with keeping you alive. We'll patch up your psyche after your survival has been secured."

What was she doing with herself when she wasn't here with me? I'd thought she was in heaven, hanging out with her late husband, Walter. Were they having mob movie marathons up there? If she started talking about people sleeping with the fishes, I'd have to rethink her final destination.

She was right, though. I forced air into my lungs and then focused on moving toward the hotel, trying to appear busy. It might have the added benefit of losing Widow Herbert. Typically I found comfort in her appearances, but not the version that had shown up today.

She dogged my steps. "You can't look weak. Even *after* we know them, soft is a bad look with this bunch of shifters. This is a new world. You have to adapt or die. When times get hard, people want to ally with the strong, not hold hands with the weak."

Well, she was achieving one thing for sure—I was no longer on the verge of a panic attack; now I was trying to not yell at her and point out that I hadn't melted down into a mess in the middle of the street. I'd paused for a second to gather myself. Hardly a meltdown. Had I wanted to? Yes. Since the world had fallen apart, I'd wanted to crumble right with it every day of the week. I hadn't, or at least not anywhere with witnesses.

I might be young, just shy of twenty-one, but I felt like

I'd just lived through World Wars I, II, and III. I'd aged decades in the course of months. I was a lot tougher than she was giving me credit for.

I glared at her, hoping she read at least some of *that* in my expression. It was the best I could do with all these shifters around who could hear the softest whisper. I'd already gotten the boot from one pack for killing in a very uncomfortable and unnatural manner. Talking to ghosts wasn't going to give me a leg up with this one.

"I know, and I do give you credit," she said. "You're a tough one for sure. But you can't let yourself go soft, not even for a second."

I shrugged, her acknowledgment taking a bit of the sting out of her words. She was right. I couldn't afford to. It wasn't just my life on the line but Charlie's as well. I scanned the street, looking for him.

Charlie was on his way over to me, running right through Widow Herbert's form. I hated when stuff like that happened. It made my friendly ghost who stopped by to chat occasionally feel a little creepy.

"Can I ride on a motorcycle? I don't want to go in an ATV." Charlie was staring up at me with hazel eyes that matched my own. They were bigger than ever as he prepared to plead his case, as if this were the most pressing matter in the world. "It's almost my birthday. I'm big enough."

His idea of "big enough" severely contrasted with mine. He'd be six next week, and I wanted him to see his birthday.

"You're going in an ATV with Buddie," I said in a very no-nonsense tone. I was starting to sound like a parent, and I wasn't sure when that had happened.

"But *you're* going on a bike," he said, as if that proved how cruel I was being.

"Because they need the room in the ATVs for our stuff. Plus, I'm big. If I fall off, I have a better chance of surviving."

"Buddie said shifters have tougher bones than humans."

Figured he'd have heard about that. Considering he was turning into a shifter, his chances might have been better than mine. I didn't care. I'd begun to come to terms with this parenting thing, and I was okay with being a dictator if it kept him out of harm's way.

"I don't care. You're going in the ATV and wearing a seatbelt, and I'm not arguing about it."

Buddie walked over. He was usually one of my favorite people, especially since he'd put his ass on the line and defected from Groza and Duncan's pack when Groza was going to burn me alive. But right now, suspecting he was behind the motorcycle issue, I narrowed my eyes at him.

He shrugged, smirking a little, not one to take offense easily.

"Don't worry, it'll be fun," Buddie said, ruffling Charlie's hair. "I'll let you drive a little."

"Really, Buddie? He's five. You cannot let him drive." I felt like I was sending off a five-year-old with a seven-year-old chaperone.

"I'm almost six and you're no fun," Charlie said, stomping away from me and heading in the direction of Magnum.

First time I'd met Magnum, he'd abducted me and shoved me in a closet, but there were few people I trusted more to watch over Charlie.

"I think he's having a rough time today," Buddie said, watching Charlie's back as he made his way to their ATV. Magnum looked as if he were trying to cheer him up.

"I know."

I'd watched Charlie drag his bag out of the bedroom this morning, looking like he was losing everything in the world. I didn't care if he yelled at me for the next year. I'd be happy just keeping him alive for the next couple weeks and making sure he didn't turn into a serial killer.

Buddie wasn't so lucky. "Did you have to make me the bad guy, though? You know I don't want him on a bike," I said.

He had the gall to softly laugh. "It's not my fault you're no fun." Buddie turned as Kicks headed over. "Hey, bossman. All packed up and ready to go."

Kicks was staring at him as if he couldn't quite wrap his head around how he'd gotten stuck with Buddie in his pack. "It's Kicks. Not bossman."

Kicks wrapped an arm around my waist, pulling me toward the side of the building where we were blocked from view. I let him tug me along, my legs moving on autopilot. We turned the corner, and his hands shifted to my hips, pressing me gently against the wall until all I could see, all I could smell, was him. His scent was warm, rugged, and fresh, overwhelming my senses. It was hard enough to act normal around him when he was in the general vicinity. Being this close to him made me feel like my hard drive had been doused by a fire hose.

"Are you okay?" His eyes scanned my face, lingering on my lips so long that my heart got a jolt. With all that was going on today, maybe Kicks wouldn't realize it was him making my heart sound like it was running the Kentucky Derby around my chest.

"I'm fine," I replied, though my voice betrayed me. I

should move away, create some distance, but I stayed right where I was.

He dipped his head closer, his jaw grazing my cheek. "You don't sound fine," he murmured, his breath hot against my skin. His hands on my hips felt like they were burning through my clothes, stealing my focus.

His breath tingled my ear as his hands, still at my hips, felt like they were burning through my clothes and stealing whatever attention I was trying to muster up to listen to his words.

"Just the nerves of moving," I said, my breathing erratic as my horse was about to drop from overexertion.

He was so close I could hear his breathing, feel his exhale on my flesh.

"I'm so glad you stopped wearing that perfume," he said.

"Well, it was hard to use when I couldn't find it anymore." I didn't doubt he'd gone and raided every stash in this little town and dumped them out.

He laughed, sending a shiver down my spine before he squeezed my waist and moved back a little. My lungs felt like they could fully expand again as he took a step back toward the chaos of the move. He glanced around the building corner, but hesitated to go any farther.

"I know you thought you'd have a little more time before moving Charlie," he said.

"It's for the best." With tensions this high, and Groza showing how far she'd go to get rid of me, staying here was like living in your enemy's pocket. Any chance of cooperation had ended. There was no reason to stay, and we both knew it.

He took another half step away. "It's going to be a long day. We're going to try not to stop unless we have to."

It had been an eleven-hour drive from West Virginia to Arkansas before the world had fallen apart. Even on bikes and ATVs, it was going to be messy.

"I'll be fine." I'd sleep hanging on to the back of the bike if that was what it took. No way would I be the weak human who slowed everyone down. They'd all been nice to me, but Widow Herbert was right—there was no room for weakness right now, and maybe never.

"If you're ready, let's go." He held out his hand, waiting for me.

I hadn't felt ready for anything in years. I hadn't been ready for my mother to die. I hadn't been ready to move back to New York, for the world to collapse, or to move here. But life didn't care if you were ready. It threw out what it wanted, and you rode the waves the best you could. Some mastered the waves and some drowned, and it was up to me which one of those groups I'd fall into.

"Yep. Let's head out."

Chapter Two

WE DIDN'T AVOID BRIDGES, main highways, or any of the places that would be obvious traps. With twenty-one shifters in our party, no one seemed overly concerned about getting hijacked by a small, random crew of humans, or at least that's what I was told.

Me? I wasn't so comfortable with it, but I couldn't take a bullet as well as they did. More worrisome, I didn't know how well Charlie could. Every time we came to a bridge that looked like it had a pile-up of cars that seemed to narrow down to a single opening, my nerves felt like they were about to undo me.

More than once I saw a handful of humans ducking for cover as we came through, as if they somehow knew they didn't want a piece of us. That we were more trouble than we were worth. Thinking back to the first time I'd met the guys in NY, I guess I could understand. Even when threats weren't obvious to our regular senses, sometimes your gut instincts would kick in and save your ass.

Not to mention there wasn't a weak-looking person in

the group. Well, except maybe for me. I was smaller than even Evangeline, but I was also deadlier. That was another weird thing to wrap my head around. I wasn't the prey any longer. I was the predator.

Whatever the case, no one and nothing had bothered us thus far except for the roads. Having to slow down at different points to navigate around crashes that spanned the entirety of the road took some time. The motorcycles that curved in and out of traffic easily didn't always appreciate the mud.

Kicks raised his hand, and the caravan of ATVs and motorcycles pulled over to the side of the highway at an abandoned gas station. I was thrilled to get off and stretch my legs for a second as I looked about the place. It looked like it had been run down before the end of the world. A plaque read "Jake's Auto," but there were no other hints of a location. The last landmark had been when we'd entered Kentucky about an hour ago.

We might've been out of the state, but it didn't feel like far enough. I wasn't sure any distance would be after Groza had tracked me down, toting gallons of gas with plans to burn me alive.

I scanned the area, locating Charlie. He was walking toward the trees with Buddie.

"Don't go far," I yelled after him.

He bobbed his head in acknowledgment as he kept walking.

Buddie looked over his shoulder, clearly insulted by what I thought of his chaperoning abilities. He hadn't almost been burned alive. I was allowed to be overprotective for a while. I might decide to drag it out for a year. It wasn't quite clear how long it would last. Maybe forever.

The wind shifted, carrying with it a potent smell of the dead. It was scary how I was becoming so used to seeing corpses.

I scanned the area, even though I was surrounded by shifters with senses of sight and smell that were much superior.

"They're empty," Crackers, one of Kicks' go-to guys, yelled out from where he stood beside the pump. His mohawk looked a little worse for wear after all these hours.

"There's some in this," Kicks said, standing beside an ancient, gas-guzzling pickup. "Who's the lowest? We'll split this between them and then fill as we go."

I strolled closer to the pickup as Evangeline rolled up her bike, a tube ready in her hand. I hadn't had much time to talk to her since we'd left, but out of Kicks' pack, she'd immediately become one of my favorite people. Plus she could cook her ass off.

"Want some help with that?" Rastin asked, walking closer. "I'd be happy to help you fill your tank."

I loved Rastin like a brother and owed him greatly for backing me up against Groza. I also accepted him for what he was: a pig.

Evangeline lifted a brow. "Thank you, but I can fill my own tank." She made quick work of topping off and was quick to leave. Evangeline was a toughie, in spite of the impression her pink hair might give some.

Rastin's eyes were still on her back. "What's her story? Is she gay or something?"

I didn't try to hide my laughter. "Why? Because that's the only reason she wouldn't be into you?"

"Why else? I'm a virile, good-looking shifter." He ran

13

his fingers through his hair, as if the wind had ruined his perfect locks and *that* was the problem.

The only thing that took away from his looks was his confidence in them. Still, he had a loyal streak that ran deep. That feature tended to get hidden by the overwhelming cockiness.

Kicks was waving people over to another car that had been pulled alongside the building.

I leaned against the pickup, near Rastin. "You would think with so many dead people, gas wouldn't be such a problem."

"The gas stations used to be refilled. Even with only ten percent of the population left, they still need it for generators and motorcycles like us. It's going to get worse as it goes bad."

"Gas goes bad?"

"Everything goes bad given enough time. Sometimes I forget how young you are." Rastin laughed.

And when the gas was gone? I might not have known about the shelf life of gas, but anyone who'd seen the white, crusty stuff on the end of a battery knew that wasn't going to work out so well. Not to mention, how were we going to charge them? We'd better get to some mills fast, but then what? A battery factory? We didn't have enough people to sustain the kind of infrastructure and manufacturing we'd had.

"Now what?" Sometimes I spend my days just trying to survive. Other times, when I got stuck standing still for a few minutes like now, reality hit hard. This wasn't a bump in the road or something we'd get past. *This* was life.

He waved his free hand, as if we were all just throwing darts in the dark. "Hell if I know. I might have lived longer than you, but this end-of-the-world shit? This is everyone's first rodeo."

"Let's get on the road again," Kicks called out.

———

As the sun set, the smiles and fist bumps of the morning were quickly shifting to groans and frowns. I leaned against an old Caddy, my hands shoved in my leather jacket, hoping no one would notice my skin was about frozen. Kicks was attempting to fill our tank for the fifth time in three hours. Several others worked their way along the highway to see if there was any other gas to top off with.

Crackers walked over. "The gang is getting a bit rough around the edges. They want to know if we're stopping at Bri's."

His attention flickered to me, and back off me even quicker. That was all it took to tell me that somehow *I* was a deterrent to us stopping.

"I wasn't planning on it," Kicks said, not looking at me.

Crackers was visibly struggling to not look at me now. "The gas situation is worse than we expected. Bri's would be a nice break, since we're going to have to stop somewhere at this rate."

Evangeline walked over, her ears perking up at the mention of Bri's. "We're only an hour or so from there," she said, giving that same glance in my direction that Crackers had.

"Is there some reason I'd be a problem? Do they not like humans? I can crash somewhere else for the night." I looked at Crackers and Evangeline and then settled on Kicks, and his body visibly tensed at the suggestion.

"No, being human isn't an issue," he said. "We'll head to Bri's. It makes the most sense." Seeing the looks shooting back and forth, there was clearly some issue no one wanted to discuss with me.

Crackers turned around, announcing to the group, "We're going to Bri's."

There were a few nods, but it seemed as if everyone had already been listening in to the conversation, as usual.

Kicks finished up with the gas, not saying anything, but I wasn't walking into this situation blind. If the whole pack had to overhear our conversation, I didn't care. They already seemed to know more than me anyway.

He tucked the hose into a bag on the bike. "There's a creek nearby. Do you need to refill your canteen and freshen up?"

"Yes, I do." I grabbed my full canteen, hoping no one else decided to join us.

We weren't that far from the group but enough to gain some privacy, especially with the sounds of water. I knelt by the creek, my back to him as I was deciding on the best angle of attack. He hit me with the true problem before I had to ask.

"I have some history with the female alpha over there," he said.

I froze, but just for a second. I was quick to recover, dipping my canteen in the stream as his eyes seemed to be trying to take in every little twitch.

Was this a recent history or something from a decade ago? Was I walking into the pack of a current girlfriend and yelling, "Surprise, look who's here?"

"Was it like a one-night stand kind of deal?" *Please, let that be the case.* I'd just barely gotten out of a messy situation, and I didn't want to walk into another. It was enough to make me want to write off getting involved with anyone ever again, no matter how much they might ooze sex and testosterone. I was at my limit for messy.

"It was more than that, but nothing too serious."

I was on my feet, trying to appraise that answer. There was a lot of room for interpretation, but even the middle ground made me feel like a chipmunk trying to swallow a cantaloupe whole.

"So you were at least like…" I couldn't get the word out. It was just the idea of another woman touching him that seemed to make my brain misfire.

"Dating her?" he offered with a shrug.

"I was trying to think of a different word, but yes, I guess if that fits." That word was the cantaloupe that was choking me. "Dating" sounded a lot more intentional, and we were definitely getting into messy territory now.

"That's probably how I'd describe it."

That was it. No other explanation on how long it had lasted? Was that because it was still going on? Exactly how messy was this?

I wasn't an idiot. He was a grown man. Of course he'd had sex before I showed up. I just wasn't expecting to encounter a situation like this on the way. Attacks? Sure. Ambushes, maybe a death or two? That too. But not this, and I needed a second to adjust to the fact that we were going to have a sleepover at his girlfriend's house.

"But you two broke up?" I asked, praying this was going to be a *yes*, and he'd provide a timeline that went back at least a couple of months.

"We were never official enough to have a breakup. With the distance and all, it made things tougher. Then of course

Death Day complicated it further." He was leaning against a tree, as if this weren't a problem.

"So where did you leave it? Is that door still open?" I tried to keep my voice calm, but was pretty sure I was beginning to lose that battle.

"Obviously not at this point, but it's something that's going to need a conversation. I haven't talked to her since our situation changed."

"And you're going to have this conversation with her when we show up out of the blue?"

This entire situation was beginning to feel like a toddler using finger paints to make a Jackson Pollock painting.

"I don't think it's going to be avoidable, considering I'll be walking in with you." He threw up a hand and headed toward the stream.

"What if you weren't walking in with me? Then what? Would you still tell her?"

He stiffened, stopping to look me squarely in the eye. "I'd still tell her about you. Although I'm not quite clear on how to explain this situation, since I don't even know what it is. Since you're so interested in labels, do you care to enlighten me as to what you consider us?"

I didn't want to have this conversation, but I would. It was hard to avoid after my line of questioning.

"Why didn't you take another mate before me?" I asked.

"Because I didn't want to. I wasn't in love with anyone."

A flare of hope burned in my chest. He'd never spoken of feeling to me, but maybe there was something?

"But you weren't in love with me, and you took me as a mate."

"Our situation made sense. I wanted a guide, and you needed a better pack to be with."

"Yes, I guess that's logical." Definitely not the stuff of fairytales, but sensible enough. What else could a girl ask for but a sturdy match that kept her alive?

I didn't have a right to be mad. He'd made a logical decision. At no point had he said, "I've chosen you because I want *you*." He'd always been truthful, more so than Duncan had. I shouldn't be mad, and yet I wanted to leap on top of him and start whaling on him. I turned into the corner and crossed my arms to keep from punching him.

He walked closer. "We can still make this situation work for both of us if you want it to. Are we even going to try to make a go of it, or is this it?"

A go of what? He'd just confirmed what this was for him, and he thought it would be cool to bang each other on top? More convenient for him?

"I'm sorry if I'm taking a little longer than you to figure out what I want. I guess this isn't exactly what I was expecting my future to look like." My voice was as bitter as coffee sitting on a burner for five hours. I couldn't seem to tone it down, even as I saw him jerk back slightly.

"With me?" he said, sounding like his brew was a bit overdone as well.

It wasn't him. He was perfect as far as men went, if he cared about me at all beyond wanting a convenient partner for sex. The idea of asking him if he could possibly ever love me, or have any deeper feelings, was so distasteful I'd rather choke on my own vomit.

He nodded, as if my silence had said it all. My *silence* was just the tip of the iceberg buried in a whole lot of salty waters.

He took another step away from me, his back rigidly straight. "This isn't what anyone expected, and whatever works for you, I'll deal with it. But I need to know where we stand."

That was the problem. I didn't want to pretend we were more than we were, blissfully walking along into a briar patch where I got caught but he didn't.

"I guess... I don't know. I guess..."

"Pips, spit it out. I'm not a lovesick teen with blinders on. I'm trying to see where we're at, and I'll deal with whatever the situation is." His voice was nearly cold.

"You needed a guide, and I needed a safe harbor. We get along fine together, so maybe we should leave things as they are? Why mess up the situation? Just be discreet in your actions." *Fine together.* That was what we were. They suddenly felt like such ugly words. How many times had I been absolutely horrid, my world falling apart while I watched my mother slowly fade away, and said I was fine? The whole conversation made me want to empty my guts out on the forest floor.

I waited for him to reply, a small, hopeful seed buried in my chest hoping he'd put up a fight, say that no, he wanted more.

"However you want to proceed is fine," he said.

There was that dirty little word again. It didn't matter to him whether we were truly together or not.

"Then I guess we know where we stand."

He shrugged, looking a little stiff. Did he want something more? Was that a sign of disappointment?

He shifted his head and cracked his neck. Yeah, all he probably wanted more of was a comfortable sleeping situation.

He barely waited for me as we walked back to the group.

Chapter Three

WE RODE down a long lane until we pulled up to Bri's pack. The place was quaint, with small cottages scattered about what appeared to be plenty of farmland.

There didn't seem to be a patrol so much as a few people hanging out near the main road that led in. They didn't even stop us—Kicks merely waved as we passed.

He drove into the heart of the small community. I got off the bike as soon as we stopped, already feeling the awkwardness of the situation pressing down on me. It would be worse when he disappeared later on, or maybe not even that late. He might disappear as soon as he saw her. After all, I'd just told him *we* were nothing more than a business relationship, and he had a history with this woman.

I kept reminding myself there was nothing really between us. Whatever he did shouldn't bother me. He'd told me on different occasions he wasn't going to be celibate for the rest of his life, and I didn't blame him. We'd both gotten into this with our eyes open, but I wasn't going to be his sex partner of convenience.

No matter how much it bugged me if he made his situation with Bri obvious, I wouldn't cling to him. He'd do whatever he wanted anyway.

I took a few steps away from the bike, giving him the space to handle this however he liked, putting whatever spin he wanted on it. There were already plenty of eyes on us, people who'd seen me get off his bike and were questioning who I was. That would be easy to downplay, explaining to her that this was a mating of convenience. Our body language would speak much louder than any words ever could. If I put space in between us, then I might be able to get out of here with my dignity intact—at least somewhat.

I slipped deeper into our group as hellos were being made, old friends coming out to greet friends they hadn't seen in a while.

I'd never seen Bri, had never heard her name before today, but I knew her as soon as I saw her. She had black hair that went nearly to her waist and seemed to flow behind her, as if even the wind was bending to her will. She had a firm, tight body and didn't look like she spent much time sitting. She wore old jeans that should've been dumpy but clung to every firm curve. Even the flannel she had on seemed to stretch tight in all the right places and then hang loose in such a way that she looked better than most models I'd seen in a lingerie spread.

Her eyes landed on Kicks and lit up. Her pace quickened as she moved toward him, a smile on her face.

With his back to me, I wasn't able to see the matching smile and was glad for it.

"Bri, I'm sorry I didn't give you any warning we were coming. We were on our way from Groza's and the ride took longer than expected." Kick's voice carried easily in the area, even as I tried to ignore the lovers' reunion.

It was like walking into Groza's pack all over again, except this time I was ready for it. The only difference was that Kicks hadn't had me ride in with Buddie, and this time I was more prepared for what was to come.

"Of course you know you're welcome. I'd be upset if you didn't stop by," she said.

Her voice was as lovely as her face, and yet her words felt like a wasp nest attacking me. Had he stopped here on the way to Groza's? He probably had. It sounded as if this was their regular routine.

"I wanted you to meet…"

He was still talking as I tried to weave my way behind Rastin, who was nice and tall and broad. He'd be easy enough to disappear behind and would find it amusing enough to not move. It was either going to be him or a bush. He rolled his eyes as I ducked past him.

I mouthed, *Shut up.*

Rastin looked as if he wanted to laugh but held back.

Either way, it didn't work, as a hand wrapped around my wrist a couple seconds later. Kicks was tugging me out of the group. The instinct to resist came and fled as the idea of a worsening spectacle entered my mind.

He tugged me until I stood beside him staring at Bri, who looked as if she'd just stepped out of a salon. Meanwhile, I'd been on the back of a bike for the last ten hours. I tried to nonchalantly run a hand through my mass of knots, afraid to look down and see how dusty and dirty my clothes were.

"This is Piper. She's my mate." Kicks somehow managed to introduce me in a tone that sounded apologetic

25

toward her, and yet not quite remorseful enough to make it seem as if he were sorry about me. He walked a razor's edge and didn't even catch a nick.

Bri's eyes flared, but only for a millisecond.

"It's nice to meet you, Piper," she said. "I guess congratulations are in order."

She held out her hand and smiled as if it were genuine. I waited for a swell of anger to rise, but it didn't come. There didn't seem to be any signs that she'd be trying to stab me later on tonight.

"Thank you," I said, trying to appear as collected as she had, but instead sounding like I'd just choked on a fly.

"I appreciate your hospitality," Kicks said.

I interpreted that closer to, *Thanks for being nice to my new girlfriend now that I've dumped you in the most awkward of ways.*

"You know you'll always be welcome here. Never doubt that."

I translated that to, *The door is always open if you want to come back.*

Even still, she'd taken the one-eighty and hadn't even gotten a crick in her neck. This chick was good, and seemed almost as smooth as Kicks. The connection was making a little too much sense. They were like two sides of the same coin.

She looked behind us, as if doing a head count. "Let me get you all settled, but then afterward, I'd like to touch base on how things went at Groza's." She looked to me and back to Kicks, adding, "Unless you're too tired, and then we can catch up tomorrow."

"No, that's fine. Let me go wash up and I'll come find you," he said, not taking the out she'd provided him.

He had to wash up to talk to her? He couldn't do it as he was? Maybe that was why she wasn't salty. Perhaps what had just been said had been for *my* benefit.

It didn't matter. It didn't.

We'd established we weren't anything more than a business arrangement. I shouldn't be jealous. I had no right to be jealous.

"I won't keep him long," she said, smiling.

I smiled back. She wouldn't keep him long? In other words, did she think she could if she wanted to? Of course she did. She actually *had* a relationship with him, as opposed to me, a business partner.

"The east cottage is open. Why don't you and Piper take that? The rest of your people can spread out in the front guesthouses and overflow into the community bunkhouse."

"That'll work well."

"I can't wait to hear what went down with Grossa," Bri said, laughing. "I told you that would never work."

"I tried to go in with an open mind," Kicks said, shrugging.

"No, you didn't. You went in with your own plan and to see what they were up to," she said, still speaking through a smile.

Kicks smiled back at her, looking way too cozy.

"I'm going to go grab Charlie," I said, edging away from them as if I was distracted and not trying to escape their too-friendly banter.

It was a natural enough excuse to get away because it was what I'd do anyway. It just gave me the benefit of not having to stand there with them a second longer. Kicks might've introduced me as his mate, but I was the third

27

wheel with a duo who clearly had a long history, and a good one.

Charlie was rubbing the sleep from his eyes, sitting on Buddie's shoulders not far away.

"We're going to bunk with the guys in the guardhouse," Charlie proclaimed loudly, and then yawned.

"You sure? Maybe he should come with me," I said, shifting my attention to Buddie. I wanted to grab Charlie off Buddie's shoulders and drag him with me, and not for his benefit. The little guy came in handy as a buffer at times.

"He's fine. We're having a guys' night," Rastin said as he walked over, smiling at me like he knew exactly why I wanted Charlie with me.

"Yeah, a guys' night," Charlie proclaimed, smiling wide.

His mood was so much better than this morning that I smiled and nodded. It wasn't like he wouldn't be safe with the two of them. It wasn't fair to make him come stay at the cottage only to put space in between Kicks and me. I might not need space. How did I know he'd even spend the night there with me?

Kicks was next to me a moment later, our bags in hand. "Ready?"

I nodded.

We walked toward the cottage, pausing intermittently as people stopped to say hello and catch up for a minute. The chitchat made the ten-minute walk to the cottage closer to a half an hour, and we did very little speaking amongst ourselves.

The cottage was a cute little bungalow off by itself, with a beautiful pond view. If we were honeymooners, it might've been perfect.

We weren't.

Kicks tossed our bags down. "They've got well water rigged up with generators, but not a lot. I'd be sparing in your use."

I nodded. I didn't want to speak to him about anything, not water, not Bri. Nothing.

"I'm going to wash up quickly and then go check on the guys. I'll stop by and catch Bri up, too."

"Uh huh."

I didn't need an IQ over fifty to figure that one out. He wasn't just going to explain what happened with Groza. He was going to make belated explanations on what had happened with us.

I tried to pretend I was getting settled in as he came out of the bathroom, looking cleaner than I liked, with a fresh shirt and pants.

"I'll be back in a few." He paused at the door, watching me.

"See you in a bit," I said calmly, like there was anything normal about this situation.

I didn't have a right to claim him, but that didn't make me feel any better about sending him off.

I looked at the little battery-operated clock next to the bed. Two and a half hours. How long did it take to tell Bri that Groza was a psycho and his mate killed people? I got sick of fluffing my pillows and tossing and turning. I also wasn't going to give him the opportunity to sleep in this bed beside me, even if we didn't have sex.

I grabbed a pillow and the blanket and settled onto the small rug on the floor. Wasn't quite as comfortable, and the chill was a bit tough, but at least I'd have my pride in the morning. Kicks could take the bed and there wouldn't need to be a conversation about it. He was lucky I was still in the cottage at all. In another half-hour I was going to go find Charlie's bunk and crawl in with him. If Kicks didn't care what people thought, then why should I?

He might not even know I'd left. Why was I presuming he would come back at all? That might've been nothing but lies. He didn't owe me anything.

My eyes were closed and my back was to the door when I heard him come in. I didn't *want* to feel relieved. I didn't want a sizzle of excitement over his returning. I had to fight my body's urge to roll over and look at him, ask him what he'd done, what had taken him so long, what he'd had to say that took hours.

"Are you making a point?" he asked.

I could hear him standing right beside me. Figured he'd know I was awake. He could probably hear my breathing or something. Maybe smell the smoke I was throwing off from all the suppressed rage burning inside.

"The bed didn't look that large. I thought I was being polite." I pulled the cover up closer to my chin, not bothering to look at him as I spoke.

One second I was on the floor, the next he was picking me up.

"Get off me! I'm not sleeping in a bed with you after you slept with her."

He ignored me, tossing me onto the bed anyway. "I didn't sleep with her. I wouldn't do that to you."

"You didn't?" I asked, already halfway up and trying to figure out how I was going to get around him. He was standing at the foot of the bed, waiting like a linebacker to block me.

"No. I didn't. We weren't even in her house. I spoke to

her outside. I ran into her before going to the bunkhouse to check on Charlie and the crew."

"*Why* didn't you sleep with her?" He certainly didn't look like a man who'd just had a good time. Even saying he appeared "churlish" might be too kind a description right now.

"Because I didn't want to," he snapped.

Where was the calm and collected Kicks? All his smoothness was gone, nothing but ruffled feathers left.

"But why—"

"I didn't sleep with her. Can we leave it at that?" His eyebrows were halfway up his forehead.

Had she rejected him? Maybe she was mad he had claimed a mate?

"Oh."

"Oh?" he said.

Was he really going to pretend he was confused?

"You know, it's understandable. She's certainly very attractive," I said. "It would be understandable if she was upset with you. You have to see how that would be a hit to her ego and make her less inclined to, you know…"

"I was not *rejected*, if that's what you are implying."

He turned, stripping off his shirt and digging through his bag, as if he'd moved on from this subject and couldn't be bothered spending another few seconds on it.

His mood certainly had taken another nosedive even as mine improved. It shouldn't have, but the image of him and her…

No. Wasn't going there, because it hadn't happened.

"I'm just saying if she didn't want you, I wouldn't take it to heart, as if you're unattractive." I didn't want to giggle, yet somehow it sounded like I did as I spoke.

31

He finished getting undressed and I averted my gaze, intent on not sending any of the wrong messages in any possible way.

The bed sank. "She didn't reject me. Can we stop talking about it now?"

"It's okay if she did. I just didn't want you to feel like—"

I squealed as he pulled me to the center of the bed, leaning halfway over me, his eyes drifting to my mouth in a way that made me lick my lips.

"I wasn't rejected," he said. "I didn't want to sleep with her."

"There's no reason to—"

My words were smothered by his mouth covering mine.

It was so hot and intense it was like getting hit with a blowtorch. If he'd asked me what I was about to say, I wouldn't have been able to tell him. All I could think of was the heat of his body touching mine. The taste of his mouth. His thigh slipped in between mine as he gripped my hip and pulled me closer. I arched my back, a groan on my lips.

"I love how you feel," he said, moving his mouth to my ear.

There was a banging at the door.

Kicks pulled back, a mixture of heat and shock in his eyes, as if he hadn't meant for this to happen.

"Piper? Kicks?" The sound of Buddie's voice had me jumping out of bed like I'd just been caught in a crime.

"What's wrong?" I was yelling before I got the door open.

Buddie was there with Charlie beside him.

"Everything is okay. Charlie just had a dream and wanted to sleep with you."

"Are you okay?"

"I dreamt I got lost in the woods," Charlie said.

"No one is losing you." I grabbed his hand, pulling him into the room and nodding to Buddie before he left. "Why don't you sleep here, nice and nestled in between us so you're not scared anymore."

Charlie hopped into the bed, settling in the middle as I took the other side.

"Yes, this way Pips won't be scared either," Kicks said.

"I'm not scared," I said, cuddling Charlie to me.

"Aren't you?" Kicks glanced over, the moonlight illuminating his face.

"I think she gets scared, too," Charlie said.

"I agree with you Charlie."

I pulled the covers up around Charlie and me. "I think we should all be quiet and go to sleep now."

Chapter Four

BREAKFAST AT BRI'S pack was an efficient affair. It was also fast, thankfully, because although we were seated in a larger house used for communal purposes, Charlie, Kicks, Bri, and I were all at a quaint little table together. This time I was a third wheel with luggage, as Charlie sat beside me.

Bri and Kicks were falling into the banter of people who were all too comfortable around each other, throwing out the occasional token question to me to seem inclusive. The more comfortable they were, the more I itched to get away from them.

He'd kissed me last night, repeatedly said he hadn't been with her, but the optics weren't great.

Charlie was eating some toast and glancing over. He kept staring at Kicks, and then Bri, his brain picking up on something off even as his life experience couldn't quite label it yet. He'd also been gulping down chocolate milk like an alcoholic falling off the wagon after a decade. Any minute now, any minute, he'd be my ticket out of here.

"You've got water here, too." I pushed the glass closer to

Charlie, feeling no qualms about using his bladder as my ticket away from this table.

"Piper, I have to go to the bathroom."

I sprang into action like an Indy driver getting the green light.

"I'll take you. Meet you outside?" I said to Kicks, already grabbing Charlie's hand.

"I can take him," Kicks said, getting to his feet almost as quickly as me.

Did he want out of here as much as me? It seemed like it, not that I was going to help him.

"I've got him. I'll meet you outside." It seemed like he might've been telling the truth after all. I turned to Bri. "Thank you so much for letting us sleep here."

"Anytime." She smiled and waved.

Kicks nodded, but there was a sarcastic *thanks* in his eyes.

Whatever had happened with them last night, it didn't seem like it was as cozy as I'd imagined.

I made my way to the bikes, where some of the pack was already gathering, my step a bit lighter than it had been last night or even this morning. Evangeline moved toward me like a magnet. I could see Buddie and Rastin not far behind, like they were getting towed in behind her.

"Was that as awkward as it looked?" she asked, glancing around for nosy ears.

Before I could answer, Buddie was there, speaking for me. "You even need to ask?"

"I don't," Rastin said, laughing.

Charlie, who'd been examining every bike in the lineup like he was an inspector, came back over.

"Why was it awkward? I want to know."

"No reason. Go get settled with Buddie. We're leaving soon." I gave him a little shove toward Buddie as Kicks and the rest of the pack headed over.

The sun had set hours ago as we drove up a spiraling road into the mountains. The fresh, woodsy scent was strong, reminding me of Kicks. The road was lined with oak trees that looked like they hadn't been saplings since the beginning of time. There was something ancient and almost prescient in these forests we drove through.

Buildings appeared in the distance, nestled in between the trees. Some of them looked like classic log cabins, not big enough to have more than one or two rooms each. Some were larger, as if they could accommodate a family. Others were brand new and only partially constructed. As the engines cut out, the sound of the nearby river filled the air. The community had been built alongside a long stretch of beautiful water.

Duncan had talked once about pack structure before Death Day, and how some pack members preferred being close. Others would live in the vicinity and blend into a nearby neighborhood. But when things got bad, they'd all pull back to one location, as seemed to be happening here.

The pack might not welcome me into their home, but I could see myself living here quite happily. Something about the land spoke to me, calling to me as if I were home. I'd never felt a sensation like it in my life, not even when I'd lived in California with my mother.

People were coming out of their homes, the excitement evident in the hurried footsteps across their wooden porches and the sounds of their voices. Various pack members walked over, greeting Kicks and the others and then carefully taking me in, schooling their voices to neutrality.

Kicks made a few quick introductions to people I could barely see in the dark and surely wouldn't recognize come tomorrow.

Another pack. Another round of judgments. Would they welcome me because I was a guide, or despise me for being human?

I spun to locate Charlie and found Buddie carrying him snugged against his chest. Charlie's expression was content in sleep.

"Where do you want me to deposit the little guy?" Buddie asked.

I looked about, having no idea.

Kicks pointed to a larger cabin sitting slightly higher on the hill, right beside the river. "The door will be open."

Buddie nodded and headed that way.

"It's late. Go with Buddie and you can get Charlie settled. I'll bring in our stuff. You can meet everyone tomorrow."

Every shifter in the area would've heard him, giving me an out to deal with all the introductions tomorrow. I wished there was an out that would take me into next month, or next year. I was tired of introductions to new packs, and experience had robbed me of optimism.

I walked beside Buddie to the place I'd be calling home for at least a little while. Kicks might've thought declaring me his mate meant this was forever.

Nothing was forever.

Someone must have prepared the place in anticipation of our arrival, as lamps were already burning. A toasty warmth filled the air along with the sound of crackling wood. It did my body good after riding on a motorcycle. It might take a week for my hands to thaw from the stinging wind.

The place wasn't as rustic inside as it appeared on the outside. The floor might've been wide-planked wood, but the furniture, large, masculine pieces, seemed newer. Buddie was already settling Charlie into a smaller bedroom as I peeked around, finding the only other bedroom and glimpsing at it through the doorway.

The bed was huge, and again, it had a large dresser, which looked as if it would hold a lot. My couple of items wouldn't even take up an entire drawer.

"I'm going to go see where I'm supposed to crash," Buddie said.

I nearly jumped, as if I'd gotten caught snooping.

"You can stay here," I said a little too quickly, nodding toward the couch and hoping he'd take my offer. I hadn't even known where I was going a few seconds ago, and now I was giving away the couch.

"Thanks, but I want to go get the lay of the land around here. I'll come back and crash if I don't find somewhere better." He smiled, making me wonder if he was going to be looking for a warm body to crash next to.

"All right," I said, predicting he wouldn't be back.

He left, and I hoped he didn't find anywhere tolerable. He would, though, because Buddie was pretty resourceful.

Charlie was still sound asleep when I checked on him, pulling the comforter up closer to his chin. I listened to his breathing for a few minutes then ran a hand over his head, testing his temperature. No matter how hale and healthy he was now, those memories of him still haunted me. I wasn't sure I'd ever get past seeing him almost die. I put another blanket over him before I forced myself to leave him be.

I walked out back into the main living area, scoping out our new home for the time being. The kitchen was open to the living room and seemed pretty well equipped. A quick check told me the water was running but the refrigerator was empty and turned off. I didn't know if that was a permanent situation or done to conserve energy.

I walked back to the other bedroom, the idea of going in it feeling strange. I grabbed the throw blanket on the back of the couch and settled in.

Chapter Five

I'D WOKEN ALONE IN KICKS' bed, no memory of being carried there, my bag on the dresser. He had come back to the cabin at some point before I woke, leaving a basket of muffins and some kind of sausage. Charlie was making a dent in his second muffin as I tried to swallow my first bite.

"Can I go see if there are any kids to play with?" Charlie asked in a tone that made it sound like he was afraid he'd never see another child in his life.

"There'll be kids here. I'm sorry we had to leave, but you will make new friends. I promise." If Groza didn't hate me, he'd still be there with his other friends. Sicko she was, she'd been willing to burn him alive in order to kill me. Sometimes when I thought of her I feared the anger was so thick that I had a rotten spot on my heart that would never heal.

He stared at me with those big doe eyes. "What if everyone here hates me?"

Every moment of suffering she'd caused him made me

not care if my entire heart turned black and rotted. One day I'd find a way to kill Groza.

"They won't. You're impossible to hate." Any kid that was mean to him was going to get the scare of his life. What he'd already gone through was bad enough. It was not going to get worse if there was anything I could do.

"Can we go see if there's kids, then?"

He was glancing toward the door. All I wanted to do was hide in here, where I didn't have to meet the new pack and see their inevitable suspicion.

Buddie stepped up onto the porch, and I waved to him through the front-door window. "Let's talk to Buddie first. We don't want to run out on him after he came to visit us."

Plus he'd checked out the place and the pack last night. He'd know if it was safe, had gotten the general vibe of the situation.

"Why? Where were you two headed?" he asked, walking over and plucking a muffin out of the basket.

"I want to go see if there's kids I can play with." Charlie stared at Buddie as if he'd have all the answers for him.

"Tons. I just saw them. Come on and I'll show you where they are," Buddie said.

"Go get your jacket," I said to Charlie before he could make a mad dash out of the house.

The second Charlie was out of view, I shot Buddie a look.

"It'll be good," he said, grabbing another muffin.

"I'm ready," Charlie yelled, running from his room, straight to the door, his hand poised on the doorknob like it was a launch button and his little engine was vibrating.

I grabbed my jacket, and that was all Charlie needed to launch into action. I picked up my step, not wanting to be too far away just in case there were a few little bastards down there that needed a good scare to keep them straight. He was already halfway down the hill by the time I got outside, heading toward a playground where kids were yelling and screaming. It would be visible from the house, so I'd be able to keep an eye on him even if he came without me in the future.

"It'll be fine," Buddie said, keeping pace with me. "Shifters at his age are very open to others. This is the perfect time for him to come into a new community. They're looking to form pack bonds and open to other shifter children. Even as we get older, it's different with shifters. Humans might be pack animals, but not like we are."

"But he wasn't born the same. What if they sense that and reject him?" It didn't help that he had a human sister with a reputation that was probably preceding me.

"You might view him as human, but he's a shifter now. There's no human scent left on him. He might not be old enough to shift, but I can smell it on him, just as he can smell it on others."

"Are you sure? He's never mentioned that to me at all." I'd known he could see and hear better, but he could smell the way they did already?

"He wouldn't. He already realizes that you can't do some of the things we can, and I think he feels bad for you." He laughed.

"He does not."

"Yes he does. He's a sweet kid and we've talked about it. I've told him some of the ins and outs of what's going to happen and what will change."

I hadn't realized quite how much Buddie had stepped up for Charlie. I'd been so worried about moving him from his people, but the ones that counted the most had come with us.

Buddie didn't seem to notice how I needed a minute. He was too busy taking in the pack members who were walking around. I could see they were all taking our measure but would smile and nod when they got caught doing it.

"He feels *bad* for me because I'm not a shifter? Does it make him uncomfortable?" Being my brother's guardian wasn't turning out to be an easy ride.

"No. He's not uncomfortable. He said he's sorry you'll never be a monster like he'll be able to be. Don't worry, though. He said he'd protect you."

If he wasn't in the middle of a pack of kids right now, and looking as if he was making friends, I would've run up to him and given him a hug that suffocated him. Even if I never had a child born from me, it wouldn't matter—I had him, and I couldn't imagine having a better kid.

Buddie pointed to a group of boulders over by the river. It was in view of Charlie but not so close it would look like I was hovering.

"The sounds of the river cover our voices as long as we don't speak too loud," Buddie said.

Suddenly the location of Kicks' cabin held more value than a nice view.

"You've never been here before?" I asked, glancing around.

"No, but I think I could be happy here," he said, taking in the lush surroundings.

"It is pretty," I said. "What about the pack? Have you gotten a feel for them?" More pack members passed by, smiling here and there and nodding.

"As shifters age they get less accepting, but I think it'll

be okay. My New York accent might throw them a bit, but they'll get past it."

"If New York is tripping them up, I wonder how a human is going to work for them."

"You're not just human. You're also a guide."

"A guide with a very bad history. You think it'll be okay?"

"I don't think anyone is going to burn down the cabin you just moved into, if that's what you're thinking. Not if they've got their heads on right. What I know of packs is that the head steers the body. If you've got a fair alpha, the rest will fall into place or move on to a different pack." His voice grew a little ragged.

Like he and Rastin had? We hadn't had a free moment to speak of Duncan, but he didn't need to spell it out. There was hurt in his eyes. I wasn't the only one who'd gotten the snub, even if mine had been worse.

"I'm sorry I put you in such a bad spot. I know that was your family."

He shook his head. "You didn't do it. The moment Duncan told us we were going to Groza's, we all knew things would change. I'd held out hope that we wouldn't stay too close or for too long, that we'd have enough distance to have autonomy and not get swallowed up by the venom of who she is. It was a pipe dream. If it hadn't been your situation, it would've been something else that drove me out of there.

"Rastin as well. He might seem like an ass, but he's actually one of the kindest of us. He wouldn't have lasted there either. I think that's why it was so easy to leave when we did. Once it became clear the packs were merging, the end was in sight."

"It helps to know I wasn't the only reason you left."

"It's the truth." He fell silent but let out a sigh that held a thousand regrets. "I'm not mad. I'm just disappointed."

"Yeah, so am I," I said.

He was looking at me like he wanted to say something but was holding back.

"What?"

"I don't blame you if you hate him. That note that he sent you about you pretty much being a dead woman if you came back—he didn't bother to seal it or even put it in an envelope. Everyone knows what it said. He wanted to make it public knowledge."

"I know." It hadn't just been a message to me. He'd obliterated our relationship in a way to make it known to all, drawing a firm line.

How had I been so stupid to think there could've been something good between us? It was hard to think of that and not shudder over the spectacle.

"He wasn't a perfect alpha, but I never thought he'd do something like that. It's like she got into his head and twisted who he was." Buddie shook his head, as if he couldn't believe what Duncan had become. "Do you hate him?"

Everything had happened so fast that I hadn't really thought about it until right now. "He saved Charlie. He turned him into a shifter. Charlie would be dead already if he hadn't. For that one reason, I'm not sure it would be possible for me to ever truly hate him. Short of hunting Charlie down himself, I don't think I could."

Buddie let out a low whistle. "Never think it can't get worse. I've lived long enough to see what happens with people. They let the world start chipping away at them until there's nothing left of the person they were.

"Why don't you go ahead and check out the place. I'm going to hang out here," he said. "I'll keep an eye on Charlie, but it looks like he's already finding his way."

Charlie was on a seesaw with another kid, laughing.

"Thanks."

Chapter Six

I'D CHECKED out the cold house, the smokehouse, the schoolhouse, and the gathering house. I'd run out of houses and had since moved on to wandering around the massive farming area.

"Piper?"

I turned to see a woman walking toward me with a dirty apron and knees. Light brown hair was pulled up into a messy bun that was more utilitarian than fun. Still, she had a cute, fresh look about her that held a lot of charm. She was also the first member of the pack that had initiated any kind of real communication, so she got points for approaching the scary girl.

"Yes?"

"Louise. I'd shake your hand, but..." She held up her muddy, gardening-gloved hands. "Do you garden?"

"No, but I'd like to. If you need any help around here." The area looked like it had been large before and was in the process of expanding.

"We're pretty good. There's others who help me tend the

field, but we're off season so they are busy with other projects. I'm just doing some cleanup and prep."

"Looks like quite a garden." It probably had to be with the amount of bodies they had to feed. From my initial guess, it looked as if somewhere around two hundred people were living here.

"We've done okay, but once Death Day hit, everyone in the pack who wasn't staying here pulled in closer. Come spring we're expanding it out to that tree, so I'm trying to get a sense of where everything might be laid out best."

I could see the stakes she'd been marking the ground with in the distance.

"Do you have any kind of blessing or words you could offer?"

She was smiling, but for some reason, in spite of her asking, I got the sense she didn't actually think I'd give one. It made my next words hurt a little, as if I were just saying the lines she'd laid out for me.

"I'm still finding my way around that side of things."

"Maybe when you get in the swing of it?"

"Yeah, sure." Something about her initial charm was wearing thin, like a bad piece of costume jewelry left out in the rain.

"Have to say, I never thought we'd get a guide here. Lots of people talked about it, and we all wanted one, but we didn't think Kicks would ever be able to pull it off," Louise said.

The more she said, the stiffer I grew. It wasn't like Kicks had made a secret of wanting a guide for his pack. We were mated, probably in part because he'd wanted something from me in exchange for offering me a safe haven. I shouldn't be bent out of shape by hearing it, but I was feeling a little dinged up at present.

She rambled on about something, but I was having a hard time focusing. My relationship with Kicks was viewed as transactional, and every shifter here knew it.

"Piper?"

It wasn't until she said my name that I realized I hadn't heard her.

"I'm sorry. What were you saying?"

"I hope you didn't take any of my silly comments to heart. I'm sure Kicks cares about you. I didn't mean to imply that he was just with you because you're a guide. There'd have to be some sort of feeling of some kind for him to make you his mate. I can't imagine he'd completely forgo the ability to have children *just* to get you here." She shrugged, her body language at odds with her words.

The fact that she'd opened that statement up as an apology was just as farcical.

"You know, I'm just going to head back. It's been a long couple of days." I should've told her to go to hell. I wanted to, and if it was just me she'd try to turn the pack against, I would've. But I was learning Charlie had to live with all the consequences to my actions as well

"Sure. All that traveling."

"Hey! Piper!" Evangeline yelled, waving me over from the other side of the field.

"I'm going to go see what she needs. I'm sure we'll chat again." I really had to work for the smile I gave Louise, and it wasn't only to keep the peace. Damned if I'd openly show that her words had left marks.

"See you around," she said, waving before going back to her work.

51

"Hey, what's going on?" I said, joining Evangeline.

"What did Lousy say to you?" she asked, motioning for me to walk with her.

"You mean Louise?"

"Yeah, Lousy. What did she say? I could see your face from a mile away."

"I take it you don't care for her." I didn't need to ask why after talking to the woman.

"Did my evil eye give it away?" Evangeline asked. "Now what did she say? I need to know if I should go back and punch her or just trip her next time she's not looking." She didn't seem to care who heard her as we walked past a few shifters who giggled at her words.

"She was just rambling on about how happy the pack is to have a guide."

"Ha!" Evangeline said loudly. "I knew she was being a bitch."

"She really didn't say anything bad." Not outright, anyway. She'd spoken the truth, mostly. That truth, unfortunately, wasn't so flattering.

"Lousy is a passive-aggressive slug. She won't flat-out hit you with anything. She'll pretend she's being nice and then stick it to you. She probably insinuated that your being a guide was the only reason Kicks mated with you. Tell me I'm wrong?" She was giving me an expression I'd seen on Charlie more than once. The *I dare you* look.

"She didn't say that *exactly*."

"No. Just implied it. She's been hot for Kicks for a decade, so I'm sure she's about as sour as my pickles that you showed up with him." She opened the door to a small cabin. I didn't have to ask if this place was hers. The kitchen dominated the open floor plan of the cabin, with every type of pot and pan hooked to a rack hanging in the center of the room. Interspersed were drying plants, which I could only assume were spices of some sort, not that I could identify anything beyond some basil and parsley.

She motioned me to a table that took up another large chunk of space. "Sit. I've got some stuff for you to try." She began filling up a tray.

"Did they ever get together?"

"They?" Evangeline flew around the kitchen as she worked on her tray, clearly having moved on to more important topics.

"Lousy? Did she and Kicks ever date?" After Bri, the question felt necessary. Although if Bri was the standard, Lousy would've been slumming it a bit for Kicks. Then again, by the Bri standard, I was as well.

But I couldn't forget, I was also a guide. Talk about a sour taste.

"Oh," Evangeline said, and then let out a good laugh. "Could there have been a late night hookup I don't know about? Maybe. I'd never know. Date? Never. She's not his type."

"Why is that?" I asked, hoping I could hold her attention on the topic long enough to get some clarity. It seemed like once she shifted gears to cooking, it was going to be a battle to drag her back to the Kicks subject.

She straightened from where she'd been bent over her tray. "You mean other than the whole passive-aggressive slug thing? She's cute and all, but he doesn't like sneaky people. Or maybe that's only my feelings? I really don't know, but it seems like he's never gone out of his way to be around her. He's nothing like how he is with you. When you walk in a room, he goes deaf to everyone else."

"Really?" I leaned back, feeling like I must have misheard her.

"I'm surprised you haven't noticed. It's almost ridiculous." She put a tray filled with tasting bites in front of me. "Now I need you to try each of these."

"Why do I get to do this?" The array of bite-sized morsels had my mouth watering.

"Because I'd have to lock up my kitchen if I let anyone else in. They're all pigs." She pointed to a couple different cake pieces. "Start with these. I'm working on a new recipe for the feast."

The flavor was so bright and full that my taste buds almost felt painful, as if they couldn't take this level of excitement.

"They're amazing. Can I ask you for a huge favor?"

"Sure. What?"

"Could you help me make a birthday cake?" If it wasn't for Charlie, I'd never have asked.

"You want to make it?" The caution in her question was leaning toward insulting.

It appeared word hadn't just spread about my killing abilities. Or maybe my cooking had been a part of the discussions as the cherry on top when they talked about my killing abilities. I could imagine them whispering, *"Wow, did you here that not only is she a killer but"—insert gasp—" she can't cook?"*

"I mean, yes?" I said.

"How about I make it? Who's it for?"

"Charlie's birthday is coming up."

"Really? That's great! I needed a better theme for the feast coming up than 'Hey, stare at the new guide, and the alpha is back.'" She rolled her eyes as if that was old news.

"I was thinking a small affair at the cabin so no one feels stressed about coming and—"

"Nope. Has to be big." She was off already jotting notes down on a paper, clearly no stopping her.

"I really don't want to put you out." This had been a bad idea. What if no one showed? Well, it was unlikely, since they wouldn't want to insult Kicks. It would probably be okay. Plus, at the pace Evangeline was scribbling away, I wasn't sure I could stop her. "Can I at least do something for you in return?

"Yes," she said with zero hesitation. "You can go to this thing with me tonight."

"What thing?" This was definitely a bad idea.

Her scribbling paused. "I'll tell you about it later. I don't want to ruin your appetite."

Chapter Seven

IT WAS the next morning when I was watching Charlie, Buddie, and Rastin fish and spotted Kicks in the distance, making his way to the cabin. I'd woken up alone, and though there'd been breakfast in the kitchen, I hadn't seen Kicks.

He met my gaze and tilted his head in the direction of the cabin.

"Go ahead. We're good," Rastin said, following my gaze.

Kicks was by the fireplace, loading wood into it, when I walked into the cabin a few moments later.

"Thanks for bringing breakfast," I said. The whole situation was surreal. I was officially living here, as his mate, with Charlie.

"No problem." He straightened, wiping his hands on his jeans. "How are you settling in?"

"Pretty good. Thanks." I didn't know what I was, but I didn't feel settled. More like a jumbled-up mess trying to find my footing again. I was like the "after" picture on one of those cube towers got knocked over.

"What do you want to do for dinner? I usually just eat whatever Evangeline whips up, but we could figure something else out." He walked across the room toward me, getting closer and closer, looking rugged and fresh and smelling like heaven.

"I'm fine with that as long as Evangeline doesn't mind cooking for us, too." This was my life now? Him? Me? Here together planning dinner? What happened when Charlie made more friends and I lost my buffer completely?

"She doesn't just cook for me. She puts out a spread in the main hall, and people swing by and grab whatever they want. I'll just pick up enough for all of us."

"She doesn't mind?"

"Mind? No. She's got assistants and waitstaff. She gets to spend her days playing with recipes and doing what she loves. We all get to eat well. It's a win-win."

He reached out, touching the collar of the flannel I was wearing. For a second, I thought he was going to cup the back of my head and pull me in for a kiss. The thought alone, and the fear he could sense it, was enough to make my skin turn red. I saw him fighting a smile, and my face grew redder.

"I have to get something out of the bedroom," I said, trying to put some space between us before he sensed anything else.

He followed me in. "I can bring you into one of the nearest towns to grab some new clothes. Feel free to take whatever I have that you can make work."

That would be slim pickings, considering how much larger he was.

"I'm actually more concerned about finding a gift for Charlie." His birthday was fast approaching, and getting presents these days wasn't so easy if you didn't know how to drive a motorcycle.

"One of the pack members is a train enthusiast. If you want, I'll see if he'll trade for one of his trains." He was leaning a hip on the bureau, watching as I pretended to look for something in my bag.

"Really? That's great. What do you think he'd want?" All I had were the few things in my bag.

"I'll handle it. Don't worry about it."

"Thanks," I said, sounding as awkward as I probably looked. The whole situation felt alien. I was the one who usually handled things.

He motioned to my bag. "You know, you can put your stuff away."

"Yeah, okay," I said.

He straightened, looking as if he were going to leave.

"I had one thing I wanted to talk to you about," I said, stopping him. "I know I said I want to keep this as a business relationship, but I'd like to keep the status of our situation private." I already knew what it was like to have an entire pack watch me get slighted, and I wasn't looking to be the fool again, publicly kicked to the curb even if I'd never technically been off the curb in the first place.

"I wasn't planning on broadcasting our details," Kicks said softly.

"Thanks. It's just that I'm on unsteady ground as it is. How many women here have you slept with?" The second I said it, I almost choked. I sounded jealous, and I was not. This was purely strategic. "Just so I know how many feathers I might be ruffling, is all."

He was good. He only froze up for a second before he said, "I wouldn't worry about it."

59

He walked back into the living room, and this time I followed him.

"Am I safe in assuming that number is more than you want to fess up to?" I asked, wondering how many more girlfriends I might be tripping over.

He sighed and then turned around. "I'm not a kid. I've been around for a while, and I enjoy sex. Have I slept with some of the women here? Yes. Of course I have."

"From what I'm seeing, you've had a lot of takers." There was no way that list was short. I didn't know how long it went, and I didn't want to anymore.

"I've had takers."

"You know some of them probably thought they'd win you over, right?" I asked, guessing the names of at least two of them.

"If everyone was a willing party and interested, that's where it ended. Is there a reason you want to discuss this?" he asked, because he was clearly done with the conversation.

"Do you plan on seeing any of them now? Here?"

Kicks shook his head. "I told you, I'm not planning on being celibate for the rest of my life, but I don't want to give the pack a bad impression, either."

There was one question I couldn't purge from my brain, still waiting to be asked. Nothing else to do but spit it out. "Can humans have children with shifters?"

"As far as I know, it's happened a handful of times, but only when the offspring somehow doesn't have the shifting gene and the baby is, for all intents and purposes, a human baby. Shifter gestation times are about twice the length of humans'."

I bit my lower lip, contemplating the implications. He'd wanted a guide badly enough to forgo having kids? Even though this was a business arrangement, I hadn't quite thought out that aspect until Louise.

"Did you want kids?" he asked gently, his eyes searching mine.

"I've already got one. I might not have birthed him, but he's as mine as it gets. I was thinking more about you. Did *you* want to have kids?"

"I thought I'd be sharing Charlie, unless you're planning on hogging him?" Kicks replied, a faint smile touching his lips.

"I just thought you'd want one who was…you know, more yours?"

"I'm going to protect him, feed him, shelter him. How much more mine could he get?"

"It's just that maybe this situation isn't right for you. I can still stay on as the guide here, but maybe you…" My words trailed off as he stepped closer.

"Oh no, we aren't going there again," he said firmly.

"Is that why you never mated before? You didn't care if you had a child?" I asked, finding that I couldn't seem to shut myself up all of a sudden. It was like I'd broken the seal on uncomfortable questions and now couldn't stop myself.

"I did have a mate. She passed away only a few months after we were mated." The way he spoke, it was as if every word of that sentence hurt to speak.

"Oh. I'm sorry. I didn't mean to pry." The weight of his words hung in the air, and I suddenly found myself silent again. I wasn't sure why, but I'd assumed I was his first. Maybe it was what I'd wanted to believe.

"You're not. You should probably know these things," he said.

"Thanks." For a business partner, I wasn't sure I was

entitled to know much of anything about his private life. The way he was staring at me right now, though, didn't feel very businesslike.

Kicks nodded toward the door. "The mill isn't working right, so I have to head over there and help them fix it. I'll be back around sunset with dinner."

"Sounds good," I replied, trying to sound more removed and aloof.

He walked toward the door but then stopped briefly in front of me, leaning down and grazing his lips over mine. It was just a soft touch before he straightened.

"See you in a bit," he said, leaving me gaping as he headed toward the door.

"Wait," I said, finally unknotting my tongue before he managed to get away.

"What?" He looked at me as if he had no idea what I could want.

"What was that?" I asked, my fingers going to my lips.

"A kiss goodbye?" he asked, his brows knitting as if he still didn't see the problem. "It was a peck. It's best to get in the habit of such things so we don't look awkward in public."

Accusing him of trying to seduce me would sound too stupid aloud, so I came at it from a different angle. "Just so the lines are clear, this is all for appearances?"

"Of course. You didn't think a peck on the lips was my trying to seduce you?" He smirked, as if that was the silliest thing he'd ever heard, then took a couple steps back toward me. "I can give you a demonstration of what I'd do if I was trying to get you into bed."

He was less than a foot from me, smiling as if he'd be more than happy to prove his point. I didn't doubt he could. I'd had his kisses before and knew what they could do.

I backed up. "No. I just wanted to make sure we weren't blurring the lines. I'm good. You should head to the mill. They probably need you."

———

Evangeline walked determinedly toward me as I left the cabin.

"What are you up to?" she asked, stopping right in front of me

"Nothing really. I was just—"

"Good. I need you to come with me." She took a few steps and then waved her hand, as if I weren't following her quick enough.

"What's wrong?" I asked.

"Nothing is wrong, but now that I'm back, I usually attend this afternoon tea thing we do. I thought you should come, you know, being the alpha's mate and also the new guide. It'll give you a chance to get to know some of the women here before the party."

"Oh. So it's a luncheon kind of thing? I mean, if everything was normal?" I immediately wanted to run. Could I use Charlie as an excuse? He was still fishing and probably would be for hours. Still, maybe he needed me?

"Yes, exactly," Evangeline said. She was looking around as if she wanted to go anywhere but where we were headed, making my steps slow.

"Did they ask for me to come? I don't want to crash the party. Maybe this isn't a good idea?" I stopped walking altogether.

"You're coming," she said, stopping right beside me.

"This is going to be bad, isn't it? Is this the payback for the cake?" The picture was starting to come together.

"Yes and yes. It's horrible. They blather on about the stupidest crap you've ever heard. That's why I need you to come." She pointed in the direction she wanted me to walk.

"So that we're both miserable," I said, forcing myself to continue.

"Yes, but I'll be less miserable if you're there, and you owe me. I'm going to make the most badass cake you've ever tasted, and it's only going to cost you a couple hours of misery."

"Fine. But why do you go if it's so bad?"

She sighed. "Because it gets awkward when I bail. Lousy, who you know I hate, is in charge of growing produce. Brittany handles the winemaking here. Fran does laundry. I blow up any of those relationships and my quality of life nosedives. It's not like it was before Death Day, where I could find a new cleaner or liquor store. *This is it*. We're *all* essential and I'm screwed. There's people I talk to now that I would've chopped off my tongue before speaking to a year ago."

"You didn't always live here?" I asked, the details of her past still a little hazy. I'd known she had a restaurant, but not where.

"No. You need to understand, before Death Day things were way different. You had lifestyle options. I lived closer to Little Rock. I had a social life. I *dated*. Then once a month or so I'd come out here, get in touch with my roots, so to speak, maybe do a couple laps around the territory. But other than that, I was living like a normie in the city."

"Did most of the pack do that?"

"It was all over the map. Kicks was mostly here because he's an alpha, and that's just their bag. If you're an alpha, you *have* to live with the pack, keep the ties and bounds strong, you know? But the rest of us... I'd say maybe a third? Half of us were scattered about, a third close but not here, and then the rest in the community. That's why all the new construction. We still have more than we can comfortably handle."

She fell silent as we neared our destination. She stared ahead as if preparing to do battle and then blew out a breath.

"Let's do it." She opened the door, and all eyes landed on us, lit up like Evangeline had brought fresh meat to some hungry wolves.

"Piper!" Louise said, patting the chair next to her. "So happy you could join us."

I took the seat like I was climbing into the electric chair. Just because Evangeline thought this was torture didn't mean it truly was *that* bad. It was all about expectations.

Evangeline made introductions around the room. In addition to the people she'd mentioned, there was also Alexa, who helped with the wine, and Margaret, who was weaving. Then there was Chelsea, the bread maker. That was such a large job it was separated out on its own, apart from the cooking. There was also the butcher, the milker, and the cheesemaker. As the list of products provided from these women grew, the picture was clear: angering any one of them could cause a bit of discomfort. I mean, it wasn't like not having cheese was life ending, but it did start chipping away at the overall picture.

They quickly launched into the recent gossip, about who at what pack had hooked up with who. Who didn't sleep with their mate anymore. They covered every topic having to do with everyone else's love life. I had too many problems of my own to worry about who was with who and when.

I'd zoned out completely when Louise turned to me and said, "You know, I wouldn't worry if it takes you and Kicks some time to settle into mated life. I'm sure you're both very tired after traveling and getting settled in together."

I sat up a little taller. "I'm not sure I know what you mean. We're settling in fine."

"You know, *mated* life. But it'll work out eventually." She grinned. "It's probably different for humans, is all."

My cheeks were burning red. I took her meaning.

Margaret, who appeared a little older and a lot more motherly, jumped in. "Honey, it's all right. We all have dry patches."

"Well, not all of us," Alexa said, giggling.

"You two are like a pair of bunnies, but it's different," Margaret said. "They were on the road. They need some time to settle in."

"You can't judge her by our standards. That's not fair," Fran said, giving each of them a scolding look and not realizing what she'd said was almost worse.

Did they assume because I was human I was a cold fish or something? Prudish and didn't like sex? My skin grew even hotter, because I *had* been avoiding sex with him.

Had Kicks said something? Did the pack know we weren't having sex? It didn't seem like something he'd do, but I'd been wrong before.

I wanted to run out of the place but wouldn't. It would just set their tongues to wagging even harder.

Evangeline, who I hadn't noticed had stepped out,

walked back in and took a seat beside me. She glanced around, taking in the silence then my bright red cheeks.

"What's going on?" she said, scanning the group.

"Nothing." I shook my head. The only thing that could make this worse was rehashing it.

She narrowed her eyes but let it drop.

I sat through the rest of the night, all guilt of Evangeline making Charlie a cake obliterated. This was, hands down, the worst outing I'd ever had, and that included having to scavenge evenings after Death Day.

I barely made it out of the gathering with any shred of pride intact.

"Sorry about that. I had no idea she'd be that bad," Evangeline said.

"It's okay. It's not your fault, or hers either if she's heard things." I wanted to vomit and then kill Kicks. Maybe kill him and then vomit. I wasn't sure which.

"Piper, not to stick my nose in where it doesn't belong, but she didn't have to hear anything. There's smells that shifters pick up on—and a commingling of smells, if you catch my drift. I just don't want you to get the wrong idea."

I froze, not sure if this was better or worse. No, Kicks hadn't betrayed me, which was a plus. But the whole pack knew if we were doing it? There went the last shred of dignity I had.

Chapter Eight

I'D GONE from afraid of falling into bed with Kicks to wondering if he wanted to bed me at all. Once again I'd fallen asleep and woken alone. Did he have a girlfriend here? A side piece? Had he already picked up with her in the short time we'd been back? He wasn't sleeping here at night, so what else could he be doing? Could I even get mad when I'd told him we were nothing more than business?

I eyed up Charlie, who was sitting in the living room and setting up the tracks of his train. I'd given it to him for his birthday this morning, and he'd insisted that it should run around the perimeter of the living room and spent a good chunk of the afternoon figuring out the best path.

"Charlie, how well can you smell?" I asked.

"Good," he said, not looking up from changing out two links of track.

"Like, do I smell different than other women here?"

"You smell like you. No one else smells like you. Everyone smells different." He held up part of his train, turning it this way and that.

"Is it because of lotions and stuff?" I said, pressing a little further.

"Just you," he said, not taking his eyes off his train.

"What about Kicks? Does he smell different?"

"Everyone does." Charlie looked up at me as if something was clicking in his head. "Why?"

I shouldn't have dragged him into this, even unknowingly. He might only be a kid, but those wheels were turning. But how did I not use his small super senses for this?

"I was just curious."

"You know, Buddie said you can't smell like us, but I wasn't sure."

"No, I can't." The tension left my body. What was I thinking? He was turning six. He had no idea what I was doing. "So Kicks doesn't smell like anyone else? He never smells like a girl?"

Charlie looked up at me, his face scrunched up as if that was the worst thing I could possibly ever say about a boy. "No."

"Hello?" Evangeline called out as she walked into the living room. "Sorry I didn't knock. We don't do that here. Shifters usually hear people coming, so knocking tends to be redundant. I'll try to do it if it bothers you."

"Yeah, I noticed that at the other pack that no one knocked much there either. I've adjusted."

"Whew," she said, her eyes widening. "That's good, because I didn't want to have to start knocking." She looked down at Charlie. "Cool train!"

"Thank you!" He beamed up at her.

"I've got some stuff for you for the party tonight," she said, holding up a bag.

"Oh. Kicks got a few things for Charlie and I figured I'd

just go like this. No?" I'd found a shirt of Kicks' and belted it like it was a dress over some pants.

She tilted her head sideways, the look on her face not hard to interpret.

"That bad?" I said.

"Not good. You really need to go pick some stuff up. We're close to the same size, so I thought I'd bring you a couple of options." She walked into the bedroom and started whipping out outfits in every color of the rainbow, all with tags. "You can keep all these."

"This looks like your entire wardrobe," I said, looking at the array spread out all over the room.

"Not even close. I was really sad after Death Day. I kept going to my restaurant every day, but no one would show up, unless they were looters. Some of them got a little handsy. I'd have to kill them, and things would get messy, so I'd go shopping afterward."

I peeked into the living room. Charlie didn't seem to care what we were talking about.

"How many did you have to kill?" I whispered.

"I don't remember the exact number. More than a few but less than ten? I always gave them a warning, but they'd look at me and not believe that I could shift into something that would absolutely destroy them. Hard to help those who won't help themselves.

"Point is, bloodstains are a bitch to get out, and I'd always pick up a few extra outfits. I did it for a while. Then I finally gave up after about a month. Might've been longer. I don't know. Those early days felt like a blur. Anyway, I've got tons of clothes. I'll drive you down into the closest city tomorrow if you want, but you can have these, so no rush."

"Thanks. I appreciate it."

71

She dragged out more outfits, laying them down on the bed and hanging some from the trim so I could see all the options.

Evangeline turned her head to the side. "Kicks is here."

A second later I heard the front door open.

Kicks walked in the bedroom and looked around. "Hey," he said. "Nice dresses." He reached up, feeling the fabric of a particularly sexy black dress.

While he was looking at the clothing, I shot Evangeline a look toward Charlie and then nodded.

"Hey, do you care if I borrow Charlie for a second? I want to show him something," Evangeline said.

"No, not at all! Take him."

"Charlie, I've got some cupcakes I want you to test out," she added. Charlie was up and running out the door with her a few minutes later.

I spun on Kicks, who was still looking over the dresses.

I choked on the words, but this had to be done, and tonight. I wasn't walking into that party without smelling of Kicks.

"Before we go tonight, won't the pack get weird if they don't smell our scents on each other?" I got the words out and they left a boulder in my throat.

"There's plenty of circumstances that can mute it. I wouldn't worry about it."

There was no way I was walking into that party without his smell. I didn't care what he said.

"Yeah, but just to be safe so that the pack feels good about our situation, perhaps we should hug or something?"

He turned, looking speechless for a second. "Are you asking me to mark you?"

"Yes," I shot out.

"It's a little more complicated than just hugging," he said, as if I had no idea what I was asking for. "There are certain chemicals that are released during sexual excitement. Hugging you platonically isn't going to do the job."

I didn't care what he had to do. This was happening. I remembered Louise's face, the gloating in her eyes, and then worse, the other women trying to make me feel better about Kicks not wanting me and the deficits of being human.

"Well, you've said you're attracted to me. Can't you just...you know?" I rolled my hand.

"You're asking me to hump your leg?" he asked.

I didn't know if he was making a joke or mocking me. The whole thing probably seemed ridiculous to him. Maybe it was.

"I didn't mean... It was just that..." I shook my head. "Forget it. It was idiotic."

"It was just what?" he pressed.

"Nothing."

"You can't insinuate there was something and then expect me not to want to know." He crossed the room, getting closer.

"I don't want to make a big deal of it, but there might've been some people inquiring into how we were doing. There seemed to be some question of our...compatibility. Forget it, though. It doesn't matter what they think." I moved away from him, taking down some of the dresses Evangeline had hung up around the room.

It *didn't* matter. I mean, yes, I was a human, and they were probably saying that was the issue because all humans were like cold fish in bed. At least, that was the way they'd made it sound, but so what? So they thought I was a loser.

"Come here." He stripped off his shirt as he said it.

73

"No. Forget it. I didn't realize what I was asking for." The whole situation was compounding my embarrassment. "I mean, it's not that I feel bad or—"

"You don't have to explain," he said.

I gave him my back, trying to see if I could make room in the closet for all the new clothes. I'd have dug through manure shit if it made me look otherwise occupied.

"Pips, come—"

"I'm going to just get changed." I'd grabbed a random dress and moved to leave the room when his arm wrapped around me.

He grabbed the belt at my waist, undoing it.

"It's better flesh to flesh," he said. "There's a certain subtlety to the scent that they'll notice."

I couldn't even make eye contact as he began unbuttoning my shirt. My heart was pounding as he slipped it off my shoulders and it dropped to the floor.

"It's not worth doing if it's not going to be believable. There's a difference in our scents whether we're aroused or not. I'm just warning you," he said, his voice growing rougher.

I didn't stop him, although I still couldn't manage to make eye contact. I was suddenly struggling to breathe, my pulse thundering in my veins.

His arm pulled me flush to him, his skin warm and hard under my palms.

We stood silently for a minute, just breathing each other in. He put his hand under my chin, forcing my head up. I forced myself to meet his gaze, and the heat in his eyes made something melt inside me. He'd barely touched me and I was already tightly coiled, craving more.

His other arm wrapped around my waist, pulling me up

higher, fitting us together until I was standing on tiptoes. I could feel his arousal pressing into me and arched into him without even thinking.

He groaned low before lifting me with one arm and cupping the back of my head with the other. He angled his mouth over mine, and my last coherent thought fled. All I could do after that was feel the intensity of our connection. My back hit the wall as his hips pressed into me, simulating the act of entering me, and I still couldn't get enough, wrapping my legs around his waist.

I was on the brink of losing all control when Kicks stiffened. He turned with me and I fell backward onto the bed, startled as he headed out of the room and shut the door.

"Hey, Charlie, how were the cupcakes?" Kicks said in the other room.

"Great, but I wanted to get back to my train."

Chapter Nine

WE WERE WALKING out of the cabin, on our way to the party, when Charlie said, "He still smells like a boy, but now he smells like you, too." Then he looked directly at Kicks and added, "Piper asked me if you smelled like a girl. Don't worry, because I told her you didn't."

"I was just trying to understand how different his sense of smell was from mine," I said.

"Yeah, she wanted to know if everyone smelled different and if boys smelled different than girls."

Okay, Charlie hadn't *meant* to throw me under the bus. I'd have to let him live to see his next birthday.

"And if you ever smelled different, like a girl."

"Well, thank you for that," Kicks replied. "It was quite a favor you did me. Can't imagine how your sister would've handled it if I *did* smell like a girl."

"Girls aren't that bad. She probably would've been okay with it," Charlie said.

"I'm not so sure about that, but I guess we don't have to find out."

I wanted to crawl under the nearest bush. I would've if that wouldn't make me even more of a spectacle. Still, I was a beacon of flashing red light with my cheeks glowing.

"I think that came out differently than what I asked him," I said. *They'd better have wine at this party.*

Charlie faced me with a small look of indignation. "But that's what you said."

"Okay, well, it's not important right now. We have to get ready to go to your party."

I tried to focus on the gathering hall, the largest building in the community, up ahead. They'd hung glowing lanterns all along the porch, warm and inviting. It had almost a magical appearance.

It wouldn't matter how beautifully they'd decorated if the place was empty. I couldn't see a body through the window as we approached, and the only thing I heard was the sound of the river running nearby.

We should've had it at the cabin. Why had I agreed to let this be a huge affair? What if no one showed up and Charlie was sitting there in the middle of an empty room? *On. His. Birthday.* My parenting tally sheet was really going to take a hit with this one.

My palms were sweating as Charlie, Kicks, and I walked up the stairs. Everyone had been invited, but I didn't know how many would actually come. Evangeline had insisted on preparing as if the whole pack would show up, and now we'd have nothing but wasted food.

We walked in the doors and suddenly bodies were jumping up from behind tables, partitions, and walls, yelling out, "Happy birthday!"

Charlie's smile was so wide it nearly split his face in two.

He looked up at me. "They're all here for me?" he asked, as if he couldn't believe that so many people would come for his birthday.

"Yes. It's your party. Who else would they be here for?" It was a battle not to cry from happiness. I'd been terrified of coming here, being accepted, having Charlie accepted. Yet they were all here, celebrating my child's birthday.

Coming here was the right choice. I'd finally found him a pack that he could grow up with. We were home. It would be okay.

"Let's greet your guests," I said to him, although I wasn't sure where to start. I didn't know most of the people here myself.

Kicks stepped closer, holding out his hand to Charlie as I hesitated. "Come on, we'll do it together," he said.

He glanced back at me when I didn't move to go with them.

"I'm good. You two go ahead." Charlie was a shifter now. I wanted the pack to see him as one, without the reminder of his human sister always there. I wanted them to embrace him the way they'd never accept me.

Evangeline popped out of the crowd and appeared by my side before I'd stood there alone long enough to feel awkward.

"I told you we'd need lots of food." She leaned a little closer, her nostrils flaring. "Wow, how long and hard were you two going at it?"

"What do you mean?" I said, glancing around, hoping not too many people were listening to this. It was one thing for them to believe Kicks wanted me and another to have the whole place think we were banging like bunnies.

"You and Kicks have obviously found your groove and worn it out pretty good." She laughed.

I'd wanted his scent, but could he have overdone it? I scanned the crowd to see if anyone was looking at us.

"Don't worry," Evangeline said. "With this much talking and noise, it makes it hard to single out one voice." She stared at me as if waiting for details.

"You could say we had a moment." That was all she was getting. There was no way I was divulging the lows I was stooping to.

"That must've been one hell of a moment. You guys must really click in bed, because I've never smelled such a strong scent on anyone that he's slept with, ever. If you were a fire hydrant, and he were a dog, there wouldn't be a dry spot on you."

Ever? Did that include his past mate? No matter how much I wanted that tidbit confirmed, I bit my tongue. He'd loved her and she was gone. It felt too sacred to gossip over, even if part of me wanted some snippet to prove he cared for me on some level.

It shouldn't matter anyway, since we hadn't even slept together. I was getting wrapped up in my own charade.

"Maybe it just rubs off on me stronger for some reason. Maybe it interacts with humans differently."

"Nope," she said. "It's actually the reverse. Humans don't hold on to the scent as well. The only way you could smell that strongly of him is if he's utterly obsessed with you. I wish I had a guy as interested in me as he must be in you." She fell silent, her forehead furrowing as she sipped a glass of wine.

I grabbed a glass off a nearby tray, feeling the need to

join her. The more she said, the more of a con artist I felt. I was going to have to tell her when we were alone.

"Come on," she said, motioning to the room. "I'll introduce you to everyone you haven't met yet so they don't have to crane their necks from across the room and pretend they aren't staring."

At least half the pack was in the building, and the other half was lingering out on the lawn. I'd already forgotten the names of most of the people I'd said hello to. I spoke to so many people I barely had a chance to eat. By the second hour, no one was looking at me weird or hesitantly anymore. It was as if they'd taken my measure and decided what they'd heard couldn't be true. I was no longer a monster.

I'd gotten cornered by an older couple asking me questions about what New York was like before Death Day when Evangeline called out from the center of the room, "Everyone! It's time for the cake!"

A path was made as two shifters carried out a large cake that would put the most over-the-top wedding to shame. It had three different tiers, with a train running up tracks around it. It was lit up with six candles that looked as big as small logs. Evangeline didn't seem to do anything small.

Charlie ran over from where he'd been playing with his new friends as we all gathered around the cake.

His face was pure joy, and then a little worry line marred his forehead. "Where's Piper's candles?"

"I don't need candles. It's your birthday, Charlie. Go ahead, blow them out." I would've blown them out for him just to move the attention back off me.

"But we were supposed to have our birthdays together?" he said.

"But this one is yours." We'd obviously inherited the same stubborn gene.

"Don't worry. We'll do something for your sister's birthday too," Kicks said from behind me.

Normally I sensed his presence like I had a built-in sonar, but the crowd must've thrown me off.

Charlie smiled, as if he had every confidence that Kicks would handle it. He blew out his candles and the room cheered. Then someone handed him a present, and then another, and I was beginning to think this night would never end.

About halfway through the present openings, Kicks grabbed my hand, pulling me along after him out the back of the building.

"Why didn't you tell me about your birthday?" he asked, his hand still wrapped around mine.

"It wasn't important. It's not even that close to his." I took a step away, and he pulled me right back.

"I think it is. When is it? If you don't tell me, I'll just ask Charlie. I bet he tells me." He was smirking in a way that made my insides go soft.

I sighed. "Three weeks from now." He might only be six today, but that kid's memory was a vault. The only reason I'd been keeping track of the days was so I didn't forget Charlie's.

"We need to mark the day, and before you try to get out of it, it'll upset Charlie if we don't." Kicks moved a hair closer, his eyes locked to mine until they dropped to my lips. His hand curved around the back of my neck as his head dropped closer and he breathed deeply. "I'm becoming nearly obsessed with your scent."

Would it be so wrong if we did enjoy ourselves a little?

Maybe I was riding a high from the night going so well and it was making me unrealistic, but at this moment, I wanted him to kiss me.

"Piper? Are you out here?" Evangeline called from around the corner. "Oh, come on! You guys have been busy enough, and you're sneaking out at a party now too? Sorry, but she's mine." She was almost in between us, and Kicks stepped back. "You have to meet Zetti. She's been waiting to say hello to you all night. She's the oldest member of the pack. Although we all love her dearly, she's not going to stop nudging me until I bring you over to say hello."

"Of course."

Evangeline grabbed my arm, tugging me along with her. We weaved our way through the crush of the hall and toward the corner, where an older lady was holding court. Her hair was still jet black, but there were fine lines at the corners of her mouth and eyes. It didn't matter. She had the type of bone structure that would make her a beauty until she died.

"Zetti, this is Piper, Kicks' mate and the new guide."

She smiled. "I'm so glad you came. You're exactly what Kicks and this pack needs in these rough times."

"Thank you. I hope so." The pressure that came with being a guide continually added to the overwhelming stress of being a disappointment. Somehow my just being here seemed to give a pack more comfort, but it was beginning to feel like a scam to me.

Zetti looked at me, and quite suddenly there was a flicker in her eyes that didn't seem to match the smile. It was there and gone before I was sure I'd even seen it. Was it actually there, or had I imagined it because my hackles were constantly rising these days? Was I seeing demons everywhere I looked? Was *I* the problem?

"Here. I brought this for you. It's been in my family for generations." She handed me a bag, and I pulled out a beautiful knit wool blanket. It was covered in a myriad of different stitches that created an intricate and beautiful pattern.

"It's beautiful." I ran my hand over the wool, sensing how precious it was. "Are you sure?"

"I don't have children, so it feels only right that it will be in the alpha's family now. It was made by my great-great-grandmother in the old country."

"The old country?" I asked.

"The tip of the Scottish Highlands," Evangeline replied. "That's where most of our bloodlines come from."

"If you ever change your mind and decide you want it back, just tell me. I'd completely understand." I tucked the blanket back into its bag, silently chastising myself for doubting the woman's intentions. I was becoming so jaded I saw evil everywhere.

"No. It's yours. Once you give a gift, you don't take it back." She pointed at me, as if chastising younger people was a usual thing for her.

"Thank you so much. I'll treasure it." I would, too. It might've been one of the nicest things I'd ever gotten.

"It's the least I could do for—" Her words broke off as a gurgling sound came from her throat.

Her mouth was frozen as if in mid-gasp, her lips becoming tinged gray, that ugly slug color of my victims.

No. It couldn't be. But as I stood there, almost as frozen as she was, I watched as that horrible color took over her entire face.

Her eyes were wide with shock and horror. She might've screamed if she could've moved her face, but the gray spread too fast. Her body jerked and then she fell over before my brain could fully process what was happening. Had I killed her? I must've, but how? I hadn't even touched her, had I?

I was staring at her body, realizing the room had gone completely silent, as if we were all in a state of shock. I could feel my body shaking.

A scream pierced the silence and everyone seemed to swarm at once, gathering around Zetti and then staring at me.

"What did you do?" a female shifter asked.

"I don't know. I don't know," I mumbled. I took a step back from my crime.

"The rumors were true. She's a monster," someone else said, not quite a whisper but almost as if they were too shocked to speak loudly.

I could hear the whispers increasing.

"They were right," another person said a bit louder.

Where was Charlie? I had to get him out of here. I scanned the room frantically as I felt an arm wrap around my waist. Even if I hadn't recognized his scent, there was only one person who would be brave enough to touch me right now.

"Magnum, get Charlie out of here. Don't leave his side," Kicks said. "Buddie, Rastin, take Piper out of here and back to the cabin and stay there with her."

"She needs to be killed," someone said.

"No one is touching her," Kicks said, then steered me toward the door. "*Piper.*" His tone was sharp enough to pull me from my panic and draw my eyes to his. His hand was on my face. "Go back to the cabin with Buddie and Rastin. Now."

I nodded, still feeling numb but knowing he was right. I had to get out of here. One glance at the crowd showed it was about to get out of control.

He gave me a push toward the door, where Buddie and Rastin stood waiting.

They were as speechless as me. Buddie opened the door while he scanned the crowd, looking anxious to get out of there. The two of them flanked me as we got outside, both continuing to scan the area as if we'd be attacked at any moment.

The cold winter breeze on my skin seemed to heighten my awareness and jolt me out of my shock. "I don't know what happened. I didn't try to kill her. I didn't even touch her."

"Were you upset?" Rastin asked.

"No."

"It was a mistake," Buddie said. "Something out of your control."

He was keeping enough distance between us that there couldn't be an accidental brushing of hands. I caught a look between the two of them. He was scared of me. They both were.

"Yeah, it was an accident. It'll be okay," Rastin added, trying to cover up the horror I'd just seen on his face.

He *never* told me things were okay. Rastin saying it was going to be okay told me one thing: this was so bad it would never be okay again.

I hadn't even touched her, but it might not matter. They were all so convinced it was me that it might as well have been.

They were convinced because she'd died the same way I had killed others.

Could it have been me? Was I getting to where I could kill without a touch? And where had Death been? If someone was going to die, I'd hear her steps. The only time I didn't hear her approach was when *I* killed them. So had it been me?

We all went silent. None of us spoke again as we walked into the cabin.

The sounds of a game playing came from Charlie's room. Magnum was in there, distracting him. How much had he seen? Did he even know why'd he'd been rushed out of his birthday?

I walked over to the couch and dropped onto it. I wanted to hide in the bedroom but didn't have the luxury of being rude to some of the only people who were currently willing to stand by me. For now, anyway. No one, not even me, would fault them if they walked away after this. I'd just killed again, or at least appeared to have.

The only thing that mattered was that Zetti was dead. She hadn't threatened me. She hadn't even hated me. She'd given me a present, and I might've killed her. I'd thought I had it worked out, that I only killed when I was threatened, but now…

I stood abruptly and then froze as Rastin and Buddie immediately jerked their heads toward me, as if on guard.

"I'll be back in a second. I just want to change my clothes," I said, motioning toward the bedroom.

"Take your time. We'll be here," Rastin said.

Buddie nodded, as if they were as eager for me to go as I was to get some space.

I moved slowly around the couch, afraid they'd run if I made any sudden movements. These men, these shifters who could become monsters, were terrified of me. They were more worried over what I could do. I shut the door to the bedroom and sat on the bed, feeling too numb to cry or yell or do much of anything.

No, not just numb. There was another feeling inside me as well—a cold chill, a bleak darkness. Was this depression? I couldn't rule it out. After what had just happened, it would be foolish to expect to feel anything remotely normal.

I sat on the edge of the bed and didn't move again, losing track of time and not caring about anything else. All I could think about was Zetti dying.

Chapter Ten

I DIDN'T GO BACK into the other room and doubted Buddie or Rastin minded my absence. I might have been rocked to my core, but they were no less rattled. I shifted from the edge of the bed to curl into a ball in the center, my mind racing. Fear was like a little monster, eating away at me from the inside out. I couldn't fathom what had happened. Every scenario that played out in my mind ended in disaster. Did I leave here? Pull Charlie from another place? The thought of taking him with me but never giving him a hug again tore at my heart. Could I leave? It might not be an option. They might be discussing my death right now. I felt leaden, unable to move even as my future, maybe my very life, wavered.

There were noises in the living room, and then the door opened. Kicks stood there. I quickly sat up as he walked in, panic overcoming me.

"I sent Buddie and Rastin home. Magnum is still playing with Charlie. I don't think he saw much of what happened."

I nodded, feeling like a coward for not wanting to face

the now six-year-old, afraid he'd be terrified of me. What if he ran from me? Stared up at me with fear? He'd seen me kill before, but after I was threatened. Not like this. Nothing like what had happened tonight.

"She's definitely dead?" She'd been dead before I left the building. I couldn't maintain eye contact and my gaze dropped to the floor. I already knew the unbearable truth. Still, I had to hear it. I had to know beyond any doubt.

"She's dead," he confirmed, his words so heavy they felt like a blow. I hadn't even touched her, but the doubt was plaguing me. Could I have brushed her fingers by accident and something within me had flared? I thought I'd seen a flicker of dislike. Could that have been enough to trigger whatever horrible thing lay within me?

"Do you have any idea what happened? Did you feel anything? Anything at all?" He walked closer.

As he neared the bed, I jumped up and moved toward the other side. "I don't know what happened. I didn't touch her." I stared down at my hands and then looked at him. "At least, I don't *think* I touched her."

His eyes narrowed as he watched me inch toward the other wall. He took another step toward me, and I backed away another foot.

"You don't need to be afraid. I won't let anyone touch you," he said. "Nothing is going to happen to you."

I tried to stop moving, stop my hands from trembling. Something about his declaration that he would still protect me, even after what had just happened, somehow made it harder to appear calm.

"I know it looks bad, but I didn't want to kill her," I said, wringing my hands in front of me.

His brow creased. "I know you wouldn't have done it

90

intentionally." He paused a moment before adding, "But if something happened, an accident, I need you to tell me."

Even he thought I was a killer. The doubt in his eyes felt like yet another blow, even though I didn't blame him. Had I grazed her? I was *so* aware of touching anyone now, so how could I have not realized? Was my power growing so strong it could pass without touch now? The thought sent a wave of nausea through me.

"I don't *think* I did." I stared at my trembling fingers, wondering what kind of deadly curse might be flowing through me.

I took another step back, but he wouldn't stop coming.

"No." I put my hands out and then immediately down again, afraid he'd walk right into them. "Don't touch me. Just to be safe. Until we know for sure. Please."

He nodded.

"I have to leave. This isn't going to be something that just blows over."

"No. I'll manage the situation here."

"If everyone, including you, thinks I did it, how is it manageable?"

"I'll manage it. It might take me a little while to calm everyone down, but it'll be okay."

My belief in Kicks' abilities was high—sometimes it seemed as if he could do anything he set his mind to—but this? An older woman bearing me gifts dropped dead with no provocation, and in a way I was known to cause. No. It was a bridge too far, even for him.

"You can't force the pack to accept this, or get mad at them for hating me," I said. "It was horrible, and the way it looks? *I'd* hate me. *You* should hate me."

"There's some explanation. We don't know it, but something will make sense of it."

The only explanation I could come up with was that I'd seen her deep dislike of me flash, and my powers had killed her. As distasteful as it was, nothing else fit. But I wasn't brave enough to voice that aloud.

There was a soft knock on the door, followed by Evangeline asking, "It's me. Can I come in?"

I was going to have to see all these people sooner or later anyway. It would be easier to start with her, and it didn't sound like she was hostile.

Kicks walked over, opening the door for her. "How's it going out there?"

"I'm trying to calm them down, but I'm not going to lie —it's not great," Evangeline said.

"Stay with her," he said, then glanced back at me, pausing before he left.

I nodded. Getting out there and managing the pack was more important, considering how ugly things could get and how fast they could devolve.

Evangeline walked in, trying a halfhearted smile before giving up the effort. It didn't go unnoticed that she had her arms crossed in front of her and stopped with a healthy buffer of distance between us.

I didn't know what to say. Everyone thought I was the killer, and even I was wavering on it.

Given what I'd done, the word "sorry" felt like trying to fix a gunshot wound with a Band-Aid. How could it do anything but make her angrier than she probably was?

"I'm so sorry," I said, not knowing what else to do or say.

"I know you didn't mean to hurt her. I could see the

shock on your face, as if you hadn't expected it." She nodded as she spoke, as if she were actively trying to reassure herself she wasn't in the room with a monster.

"I don't know what happened. I didn't touch her, but I know how bad it looks. I understand if you hate me." My voice cracked, knowing how pathetic my words were and how short they fell of exonerating me in any way.

She shook her head. "I don't hate you. Of course I'm upset over the loss of Zetti, but you're not a bad person. You wouldn't have done this on purpose. Something had to have happened. Did she scare you somehow?" She was doing mental gymnastics trying to make sense of a situation that had no answer.

"No. Not even a little."

She just nodded. It was beyond obvious she was convinced I'd killed Zetti. The only thing I had going for me was she thought it was an accident.

"It'll be okay. We'll figure out what happened and go from there," she said, her words a thin veneer of reassurance.

I believed that as much as she did. Deep down, a part of me was terrified that nothing would ever be okay again.

Chapter Eleven

I WAS LYING in bed at dawn, wearing the same clothes as last night, staring at the ceiling, when Kicks walked in.

"I've been thinking about this all night. I think the best way to approach it is to hit it head-on, call everyone over, and just put it out there."

I sat up, not liking the sound of this at all. "Put what out there?"

"That we're looking into what happened. That you had no malice toward Zetti and that you aren't to be blamed for what happened. That's it. Beginning and end of story."

I stared at him, speechless. Could he be that naïve to think this would work? He'd declare it so and that was it?

I finally found some words, and they weren't good for my case. "Except even you doubt whether I killed her or not."

"It looks bad, but *you* don't think you killed her. I believe you." He walked over to the window, looking as if he were trying to piece this together himself. "I believe, at least, that it wasn't intentional."

I hoped he wasn't planning on putting that last line into the speech. It didn't sound like a winner.

"These people don't know me enough to guess at my intentions or presume I didn't mean to murder her," I replied. "What they've heard is going to make them lean the other way. This won't work."

"They'll listen to me. They might not believe it, but they'll give you the benefit if I demand it, and I do."

I'd thought I was stubborn, but looking at the set of his brows, the line of his mouth, he wasn't going to budge. He was going to tell them what to think, and damn them if they didn't go along with it.

When I first got my mother's cancer diagnosis, I'd convinced myself I could fix her, that I'd find a way to heal her from the strength of my convictions alone. He looked as if he were having a similar moment, thinking he could force his will and make this right through sheer determination.

I'd been wrong. I was sure he was wrong as well. One of the things that held a pack together was safety and survival in numbers. If one of the numbers in the heart of the pack was diseased, the entire structure around it crumbled. Unfortunately, I was looking like that diseased limb that had to be cut off.

"I'm arranging to speak to them this morning. The sooner the better. I'll get Magnum to take Charlie up river a ways fishing, far enough away that he won't hear anything."

Charlie would hear the chatter soon enough anyway, but in case the meeting went bad, I'd spare him the worst of it if I could. Either way, there was no stopping Kicks. This was going to happen.

I watched Charlie sleep, and a frisson of panic set in when he stirred. He opened his eyes and smiled at me.

"Are we having more muffins for breakfast?" he asked.

"Sure. Kicks already picked some up." Was that his biggest concern? Did he know what had happened?

He slid off the bed, yawning and making his way to the kitchen table.

"Did you hear about anything that happened last night?" I asked.

"Yeah," he said, taking a bite of a muffin.

I poured him some water. "Are you upset about it? If you are, I want you to tell me, okay?"

"Sure," he said. "Do we have any chocolate milk?"

Did he know Zetti was dead? Did I push it further or let it go? Did I want to turn it into something for him if it wasn't? But what would happen if he didn't know and heard about it later?

"Someone looking for milk?" Kicks asked, walking in the door with a jug and one of those squeezy bottles of chocolate that had a shelf life of a decade.

"Yay! Thank you, Kicks," Charlie said.

Kicks brought the stuff over to the table. "Magnum wanted to take you fishing today at his favorite secret spot, so get dressed as soon as you're done eating."

"This is the best day ever," Charlie said, then gulped down his milk and took a muffin with him back to his room to get ready.

"Where's Charlie going to be, exactly? How far up the river?" I asked Kicks.

"A couple of miles, just out of earshot. Don't worry. Everything is going to be fine."

Yeah, there was that word again—fine. If he wanted to calm me, that wasn't the word to use.

"Don't forget you said that."

———

"Are you ready?" Kicks asked an hour later.

Ready? To see the pack who thought I was a murderer and probably wanted to hang me? Was there a way to get ready for that? "Sure."

The minute I walked out of the cabin, I could feel the tension in the air, the crowd that was forming nearby all turning their gazes to me. I took a deep breath, trying to not look as rattled as a pissed-off snake.

Kicks wrapped his hand around mine. It might've been to show his support in front of the pack, as more than a few sets of eyes went to our connection. He gave my hand a squeeze before stepping forward. The visual might've been for the pack, but that had been just for me. I walked beside him, feeling as if his hand were a lifeline, and we made our way to the head of the crowd.

The murmurs quieted as we stepped in front of what appeared to be the entire pack. The two hundred or so members felt more like two thousand as they stared at me with open suspicion. Kicks didn't let go of my hand once, not even as he started to speak.

"I want to open up by saying we're all hurting today. We're all mourning Zetti. She was the oldest of our pack, like a grandmother to most of us. Her presence was part of the foundation of this place and our people."

It made sense for him to open up like this. He had to acknowledge her death. It would be callous of him not to. Still, it made me want to crawl under a rock like the slug I was viewed as.

"By now, even if you weren't there last night, you've all heard the stories of what happened. In spite of what you might've heard, we don't know what caused Zetti's death. Whatever happened was not brought about by an intentional act. We are looking into what caused her death, but at most, it was an accident. There are things being said, suggestions being made, that will not be tolerated. I won't repeat them here because they're unworthy of being discussed.

"No one will be getting punished for it. No one will be targeted because of it. I will not stand for any acts of aggression in relation to it. That is my final word, and if you can't live with that, then you're free to leave this pack."

Kicks was standing in front of his shifters, giving them an ultimatum, while I stared over the crowd's heads, afraid to make eye contact. I'd seen their looks once, and I didn't want to see them again.

This wasn't the way I'd imagined this going down. I hadn't expected him to have my back to quite this degree when even he had his doubts. And yet here he was, telling them all they had to accept it or leave.

Part of me wanted to jump into his arms and thank him, maybe sob a bit as I did. The other part was speechless. He couldn't believe this was going to work, could he? I got it, he was their alpha, but there had to be limits even in this sort of setup, right? That part of me wanted to drop my face into my hands and groan.

"Any questions?" Kicks asked, his tone breaking through my thoughts.

No one said anything. They might have been too shocked to speak.

"Then that's all," he said as some still stared, gaping at him.

The crowd slowly broke away, little clumps of people at a time wandering off and looking as shocked as I was. I didn't wait for Kicks and wandered back to the cabin, although he was right behind me, feeling almost like a bodyguard at the moment.

This wasn't going to work, was it? I dropped to the couch, reeling even more than I had last night, if that were possible.

He was crazy. I was mated to a crazy man.

Kicks pulled out a bottle of what looked like whiskey from a cabinet in the kitchen. "Want a drink?"

I ignored his question. "You can't bully everyone into accepting me. If that's the plan, it's not going to work."

"Does that mean you want a drink or not?" he asked, then took out two glasses anyway.

"This won't work."

"I'll take that as a yes," he said, pouring two drinks. He carried one over to me and then took a healthy sip of his own.

He wouldn't need alcohol if he thought this was possible, but he was going to refuse to acknowledge the situation. I wanted to pull my hair out or bang my head against a wall. I wanted to bang *his* head against the wall until reality set in, and yet I was also having a hard time resisting the urge to wrap my arms around him. Not once in my life had another man stood up for me like that.

It was insane. His plan had no chance of working, might destabilize his very pack, and yet he'd told them in no uncertain terms they were going to accept me or get out. It was the exact opposite of what Duncan had done, and I could feel myself nearly melting over the whole situation, except for one issue: you couldn't *make* people accept others. Life didn't work like that, even for Kicks.

I nursed my drink, which I had assumed was whiskey, but now I doubted that as it burned like a blowtorch going down. Kicks sat in the chair, doing the same. I waited until he was halfway through his glass before I tried again, wondering if this foul drink might make him more open to reason.

"They *aren't* going to accept me."

He took another sip, as if stalling. "They'll get past it and move on. It'll take some time, is all."

Maybe, just maybe, he was right. Given long enough, some of them would eventually get over it, decide it hadn't been me, or whatever else they had to do to rationalize living in the same pack with me. But there was one gigantic problem still looming, and it was so bad I was afraid to utter it aloud even as my mind couldn't move off it. What about when it happened again? Then what? The way people were dying around me these days, it was more likely than not. They might turn and look away once, but they wouldn't do it again.

"If they don't?" I asked before sipping some more of the nuclear acid he'd served up.

"Where are you going with this?" His question was laced with enough suspicion that I could tell he already knew the answer.

"This might not be the right place for Charlie and me if things don't settle down." I broke eye contact halfway through, feeling like I was spitting on his efforts to help me. It wasn't like I had another place to go. This was all I had right now, but I wouldn't hang on for dear life like I did last time, waiting for things to work out when there was nowhere to go but down.

"If this doesn't work, then *we* go. I'm not letting you

leave here with a child alone. You go, I go. That's what being mated means."

"You can't leave your pack. They'll fall apart without you. You're the alpha." He led instinctively and without effort. People reacted to him, wanted to follow him, and there were at least a couple hundred people here who looked at him like he was a god.

"They'll adjust. They'll choose a new alpha, the next strongest stepping up. Probably Evangeline or Crackers. Life will go on."

He couldn't be serious, and yet he sat there with a determined look on his face. Kicks didn't offer up empty promises. He did everything he said he would.

"I can't have you do that. Give up your home for me." I finished the rest of my drink in one gulp.

"It's my choice, same as yours." He continued to sip his, as if he'd already thought this out.

Maybe he wasn't as immune to reality as I feared. Still, this was not an option. I wouldn't ruin his life along with mine. He shouldn't be punished because he was loyal.

"I think you're taking this situation between us too far. You claimed me as your mate because you wanted a guide for your pack. I agreed because it was an easier way to transition. But your pack isn't going to want a guide bad enough to keep me, and we both know they aren't getting any benefit from me." As I said the words aloud, for the first time I truly began to feel the loss. We might not be truly mated in my mind, but I lived with him, I spoke to him every day, and I was going to miss him, maybe more than I'd imagined I could.

"I claimed you as my mate. I made a commitment and declared it to the world. Just because we haven't slept together doesn't change that. *Nothing* is going to change that." He put his glass down and walked out, as if he wouldn't even hear anything else on the subject.

I used to wonder what it would be like to have someone as loyal as Kicks at your back. Now I knew, and unfortunately for him, I was an albatross around his neck. I wouldn't destroy his life along with mine.

Chapter Twelve

IT WAS the second day since Zetti had died, a day since Kicks had informed the pack they were going to either get along with me or get out, and we were all sitting around the kitchen table like nothing was amiss. Kicks, after sleeping who knew where last night, had strolled in with a basket of freshly baked croissants and an urn of coffee and fresh milk. Even the buttery perfection of the croissant couldn't distract me from the strangeness of the situation. Were we really going to pretend everything was normal after what had happened?

"Charlie, the teacher was asking about you. Are you ready to start school?" Kicks said, his voice too casual.

Yep. We were going to keep going like nothing had happened. It had been the plan to get Charlie in school, but that was before Zetti died. Did Kicks not realize the potential issues now?

"Do they have room? If they're mid-semester or in the middle of lessons, maybe he should wait?" I phrased it like a question, but my stare made it clear Charlie wasn't going anywhere until I checked things out. The condemning glares from the pack were still fresh and raw in my mind, but Kicks thought sending Charlie to school with these people was a great idea?

Charlie stared at me as he continued to eat, as if he couldn't figure out what had happened to me.

"I talked to the teacher this morning, and she isn't worried about him starting mid-lesson. She doesn't think it'll be a problem," Kicks said, trying to imply everything would be fine because they'd had a chat.

"Still, I'd like to go check out the school before he starts." Just because this teacher was nice to Kicks, the alpha, the leader who could banish her, didn't mean she'd treat my helpless little six-year-old well.

"Do you not like the teacher?" Charlie asked, worry starting to leak into his voice.

"No, not at all! I've never even met her." At least, I didn't think I had. "I just want to go check everything out myself and make sure it's good."

"That's a great idea. I've got to help at the mill, but I'll be around this afternoon if you want me to come," Kicks said.

"That's okay. Charlie and I can go after he's done eating." There was no way I was waiting for Kicks so he could taint the whole experience with his alpha presence, skewing their reactions.

Kicks nodded, a look in his eyes saying he understood.

We all fell silent again. The idea of Charlie being away from me at this point made me want to choke on my croissant.

"I wonder if Alex and Petro will be there today?" Charlie said, mentioning the two kids he'd been playing with the other day. "I'm going to go get ready." He choked down the rest of his croissant and was off to his room.

I shot a glare in Kicks' direction before picking up some plates and bringing them to the sink.

"It'll be fine," he said, following me.

"You can't know that."

"Cecelia, the teacher, is a kind-hearted shifter. You'll like her."

I wasn't so sure, but I wouldn't start this argument until after I met her.

———

The morning sun was hidden behind storm clouds, as if trying to warn me this wouldn't be a good day, while Charlie and I walked toward the school. He scanned everyone we neared with a squinty look.

"What?" I asked.

"Nothing."

"It's obviously something," I said.

"Are they staring at you because that woman died and they think you did something?" he asked, his voice barely a whisper.

"I think so." I tried to keep my voice calm even if I was anything but.

I wasn't sure how much Charlie knew, but it wasn't worth debating right now. The point was he did know, and I was going to have to get used to him hearing a lot of things with those ears that I'd prefer he didn't.

"Do you like it here so far? The other kids seem nice," I asked, trying to shift the focus to something other than the latest death associated with me.

"They're really nice," he said, wrinkling his nose as he walked.

"Then why are you making that face?" I asked.

"I can't say."

"Why not? You can tell me anything," I said.

"Because I thought I wasn't supposed to talk about how people smelled," Charlie said, looking up at me as if he were truly confused now.

"Do you mean me? Do I smell bad?" I asked, glancing around to make sure no one else was trying to listen in. Waking up and feeling like a murderer was bad enough. Now I was a smelly killer?

He didn't have to say anything else; his face crinkled up a little more.

I stank. The kid was telling me I stank!

"What do I smell like? Is it bad?" I said, not sure if I wanted to know but feeling like I had to.

"Not bad. Just different, like those white flowers."

"What white flowers?" It was winter. What was he talking about? We hadn't seen a flower in months.

"The ones my mom bought for the neighbor when her daddy died."

I smelled like funeral flowers. No. It was just a coincidence. Zetti dying did not somehow make me smell different.

"Have I smelled like these flowers before?"

"No," he said, with no hesitation.

Maybe it was the clothing I was wearing. It was from Evangeline. It *would* smell different. I could even smell the difference with my plain old human nose. That was all. I couldn't let something so simple make me crazy.

We were at the school, which hadn't yet started. The kids were all running wild outside.

"Charlie!" one of the little boys called from across the field. He had two others with him, and they were waving Charlie over.

"Can I go play?" he asked, sounding like a boy who was starving and begging for a crumb.

"Yeah, go ahead. I'll find you after." It might be better to be alone anyway, in case words needed to be said.

I walked into the small single-room building. It reminded me of what schoolhouses might've been like a couple of centuries ago, and I wondered how one person managed all the kids. That one person was bent over her desk at the front of the room. She didn't look familiar, but that didn't mean she hadn't been there at the party. Even if she hadn't, she would've heard.

She glanced up to see who'd entered her domain. Although she didn't look angry about my presence, there was a glimpse of surprise.

"Piper?" she asked.

"Yes. I'm Charlie's older sister."

"Yes, Kicks said Charlie would probably be starting school here soon. I'm Cecelia. Nice to meet you." Her smile seemed friendly enough, but she didn't make a move to shake my hand. I didn't hold that against her.

"I wanted to stop by myself and make sure you were okay with Charlie coming here. I'm sure you're already juggling a lot," I said, giving her an easy out if she wanted to take it. "I've been toying with schooling him myself, so it really wouldn't be an issue at all if it was too much." Now the groundwork was laid, she could easily back out if she had any doubts about getting involved with us. Even the tiniest hint she didn't want him here, and I'd tell Kicks I was going to school Charlie myself. It would be easier than his feeling like he had to fix a situation that couldn't be fixed.

"I've seen him playing with the other kids. He seems like a lovely boy. I think he'd fit in here nicely, as long as you want him to come."

She seemed sincere. Too bad I couldn't sniff out emotions like a shifter.

"I wouldn't want you to be put out in any way," I said, trying to add extra weight to my words so she fully understood. "It's just that children pick up on that sort of thing, and if you felt like it was too much on you, it might be better if he didn't come. I don't want there being any misunderstandings." The only way to make that clearer would've been to pull out a blade and tell her not to screw with my kid.

Her chin inched up. "I understand you don't know this pack, *or me*, but I never feel put out by teaching children. If Charlie does come here, there won't be any kind of misunderstanding."

She had the direct stare of someone willing to back up their words. I might be uneasy with the pack, but I liked her. I just hoped I was right. Too bad Widow Herbert wasn't around to bounce it off, but it seemed she had other things to do lately than haunt me.

"Okay, then he'll be here tomorrow if that's good?"

"Sounds good."

Chapter Thirteen

I FINISHED MAKING the bed I'd been sleeping in alone for more than a week now. I wasn't sure where Kicks was sleeping, but it wasn't with me. Not that I blamed him. I wouldn't have wanted to sleep next to me either. I just wished I knew where he was spending his nights. I'd ask Jaysa or Widow Herbert if they could find out, but they were both avoiding me, too.

"Piper? Are you walking me to school?" Charlie asked, standing in the bedroom door, his backpack sitting on the floor beside him.

"Of course I am. I didn't realize what time it was," I said, glancing at the clock.

I slipped on my boots and paused by the front door, spotting Kicks cleaning up the plates from breakfast. Every morning he'd slip back in after spending the night somewhere else. We'd nod or say a few words, pretending there was nothing odd about it.

"Let's go, Charlie," I said, leading him outside. The chill of the morning air matched my current mood.

We started our short walk, with the pack keeping their distance from me. They weren't throwing stones, so things were going better than they might've. It hadn't been that long since Zetti's death. I couldn't expect a miracle, but at the same time, I had a feeling it wasn't going to improve. At least their feelings didn't seem to be bleeding over onto Charlie.

If they caught his eyes, they'd smile in greeting. Then that smile would quickly fade as their eyes rose to mine.

If it wasn't for walking Charlie to school every day, I'd avoid the pack altogether, whether it was the right thing to do or not. But he liked my walking him to school, so I did. I was beginning to wonder if he was just trying to get me out of the house.

We got to the little schoolhouse, and Charlie ran ahead, already mixing in with the kids like he'd known them for years. He belonged here now. He was one of them. Even though I was a guide, I'd never fit in this place with the deaths that clung to every mention of my name. At some point, I'd have to leave, and probably alone. The harsh truth was that I wasn't helping Charlie have a good life. I was a preventing him from fully integrating into this pack. I was like a black mark on his otherwise stellar resumé. A ding in his brand-new car.

I turned to head back to my self-enforced isolation, away from the curious and judgmental eyes. My last place of peace in a place full of suspicion.

I could see Rastin watching me, heading over to the cabin with a determined step. He got there first and waited.

"Let's have a chat," he said.

"Sure," I replied with absolutely no enthusiasm in my

voice. That wouldn't be anything to deter Rastin. He was too thick-skinned to be averted by subtleties. Even a stern *Go to hell* didn't usually work.

I'd barely walked inside when he launched into his diatribe.

"There's two kinds of people in this world. You've got your ride-or-die and then your joy ride. Your joy ride is in it for the good times, but as soon as the bike breaks down, they're hopping on with someone else while you're bent over a flat at the side of the road. It's fine to have a little fun with the joy rides, but you know what you're getting. Then you've got your ride-or-die. Those—"

"I'm aware of what a ride-or-die is. What I don't get is the point of this conversation. Are you bored? Will no one talk to you here? You know, if you just tried to be a little less abrasive, you'd make friends a little easier." Unlike myself. There was no redeeming my social status in this pack.

He cleared his throat, making a point of ignoring my comments. "The point of this conversation is you don't seem to understand the value of ride-or-die people. I might not always see eye to eye with Kicks, but that man is ride-or-die. You don't walk away from someone like him. If he's willing to ride or die with you, you stick it out."

Rastin might be smarter than people gave him credit for, but no way could he read my mind. This was not a conversation I was willing to have with anyone. If and when I left, I was doing it alone this time.

"I'm sorry, but I'm still not seeing your point." I walked over to the table, but Kicks had already cleared it. The sink was also empty. *Damn.* He'd left me no distractions from this horrible conversation?

"You think I can't see the urge to flee in your eyes? You hung on with a death grip at a pack that was a dead end. Now you're looking to run for the hills when you've got people who are willing to back you?"

I walked into the living room, determined to find something else to do. "First off, I'm not looking to run for the hills—"

"Save it. You're barely hanging on, and it's very clear. We couldn't drag you out of Groza's—"

I spun on him so fast he nearly jumped back. "And look how that turned out. Look how I ended up leaving. I'm not doing that again. It was a mistake."

"Staying there was a mistake, but that doesn't mean you should run from here. Can't you see the difference?" He was nearly pleading, as if he saw his friend about to make a huge mistake.

"Difference? Yes. Other than Groza and Duncan, the rest of the pack *liked* me there. Here I'm a pariah." He didn't get it either. My being here wasn't good for anyone.

"Fine. They aren't exactly embracing you, but Kicks has your back, and leaving *him* is a mistake."

None of them saw it. Or they didn't want to. There was something *wrong* with me. Maybe a human never should've been made into a guide for a reason. There was something wrong *in* me, and I could sense it. I'd felt it ever since Zetti died. Something dark and twisted had planted a seed within me, and it wasn't going away.

"What if staying here is a death sentence for him?" It was the most honest thing I could say to Rastin.

"It won't," he said, refusing to acknowledge the threat I was becoming.

"Rastin, I'm not the girl you first met that you took out of New York." I didn't want to own it myself, but at some point, we'd all have to accept it.

"Stop that. Of course you are. Hey, it's not as if you kill the people you *like*," he said.

I didn't laugh. He mustered up only a smile, not even laughing at his own joke.

"Sorry. Too soon?"

"Yes. Now if you don't mind, I'm already in a bad mood." I waved toward the door.

"Does this mean you're done with the conversation?" Rastin asked.

"Wow, you're quick today."

Kicks walked into the cabin and nodded at Rastin, who was heading for the door. "Stay. I need to talk to you."

Guy was going to get a crick in his neck with my telling him to go and Kicks making him stay.

"What's up?" Rastin asked, already sounding guilty.

Shit. What had he done now? I couldn't leave him hanging out there alone if it was bad. He'd had my back against Groza and protected me after I appeared to kill some little old lady. Bottom line was, after someone did things like that, it didn't matter much what else they did.

"You need to slow it down or limit the numbers. It's causing me grief," Kicks said, crossing his arms and leaning his hip against the couch.

Huh? What the hell was he talking about?

"With all due respect, you're my alpha, not my nurse-maid. I'm a full-grown shifter with needs," Rastin said. His words might've sounded tough, but his tone was toeing the line.

I should've guessed this was the issue. Rastin did like to get around, even if it could become problematic.

"I don't care if you bang a new female every night, but I've got fights breaking out. You couldn't at least give it a day in between?" Kicks' tone was harsh. He might've asked a question, but it didn't seem like he wanted an answer.

"That situation wasn't my fault. I was messing around with one, and the other joined in. If they didn't like the situation, they shouldn't have started it," Rastin said, shrugging but looking sheepish. "Who has a threesome if you're the jealous type? I say that's on them."

I backed farther toward the kitchen, afraid of drawing attention to myself if I started to laugh.

"However it's happening, you need to slow it down or smooth it out. I don't want to have to clean up the messes you're making. Do you understand?" Kicks' eyes bored into Rastin. "I don't need more problems right now."

Yeah, he had his hands full with the ones I was causing. I wasn't sure if Rastin picked up on that, but Kicks' gaze shot toward me, as if he knew he'd slipped up.

Rastin shifted his weight from one foot to the other. "I can't help it if I need more sex than—"

"Don't finish that sentence." Kicks was staring like he'd take Rastin out at the knees if he said another word.

It didn't matter. We all knew what Rastin was going to say. Anyone could fill in the blanks.

He stood there for another moment, as if unsure what to do. Even he seemed aware he'd crossed the line.

"Go," Kicks said, giving a pointed look toward the door.

"See you, Rastin," I said, making sure he knew we were good despite his playboy ways and earlier unwanted conversation. He wasn't always appropriate, but he wasn't intentionally mean.

Actually, sometimes he was. *Whatever*. He was still my friend.

As Rastin left, Kicks shifted his gaze to me, his eyes softening. "I didn't mean that toward you."

"The 'any more problems'? Yeah, you did," I said, crossing my arms. It was true, but that didn't soothe the sting.

I went into the kitchen, once again trying to find something to busy myself with to avoid yet another unpleasant conversation.

It didn't work this time either, as he followed me.

"We should take a walk tonight, get around the pack," he said.

"No. I'm good." I walked past him into Charlie's room, remembering the bed was unmade. I just needed to stall until Kicks left. It wasn't like he'd be here all night. I wasn't sure where he went, but he wasn't here.

He followed, leaning against the doorjamb. "You have to get out of this cabin more and let them see you."

I kept my attention on the bed but couldn't stop myself from asking, "Is that what you're doing when you leave here every night? Letting them see you?" My voice came out sharper than intended.

He jerked his head back, having the gall to look surprised. "I thought what I was doing was giving you space, since you clearly want to be alone."

"What happened to the whole spiel about wanting to present a good image for your pack? I guess that doesn't matter anymore as long as you have a warm bed."

"I'm not sleeping with anyone here. I'm not sleeping with *anyone*," he said, his voice rising.

"Well, if you wanted to give me space, you'd be on the couch. Not missing every night, making it look like even my mate thinks I'm a killer." I threw Charlie's pillow on the bed before walking out of the room and trying not to touch Kicks as I passed him.

"I didn't want to make Charlie concerned," he said, following me.

"Sure. This is about *Charlie*," I replied, rolling my eyes.

"I'd gladly sleep in your bed, but I'm not welcome there," he said. "Even if I proved to you that wasn't the case, you'd put this wall up anyway, and we both know it." He stepped closer, his eyes locked on mine. "You jumped in with Duncan with both feet, and now you're so afraid that no one can even get close to you."

"I didn't realize you were trying to get close to me when you were crawling into Louise's bed." I knew she was willing and waiting.

"I'm not sleeping with Louise, not that I shouldn't after you told me we're nothing more than a business relationship," he said, his voice growing lower and more intense.

"You said you wouldn't embarrass me in front of the pack, or did you forget that?" I turned, heading toward the bedroom, my anger growing so thick and hot I was afraid to be near anyone, even him. I went to slam the door, but he was there, his hand stopping it from closing.

"I *haven't*."

"Then where are you going every night?" I yelled, not caring if every shifter in the pack could hear me.

"I'm sleeping in the mill."

"Sure you are." I tried to slam the door again, but he'd planted his foot along it.

"I was trying to give you space, but I'll sleep here if that's what you want."

"Don't do me any favors." I grabbed the door, shoving with all my might.

He stepped back, his hands up in surrender. "Fine."

"Fine," I said, finally getting to slam the door, but it didn't make me feel a whit better.

Chapter Fourteen

I ROSE before the sun with my thoughts already spinning. I was so distracted I didn't notice Kicks lying on the floor until it was too late. I fell onto him, hearing a grunt as my knee connected with a sensitive spot.

"Oh no, are you okay?" I scrambled off him, my heart pounding.

Kicks nodded but held up a finger, silently asking for a moment.

"It's not my fault," I said, grimacing as he looked as if he could barely breathe. "I didn't expect you to be there."

Waiting for him to compose himself, I noticed the blanket and pillow on the floor.

"You slept here?" I asked, my voice sounding smaller somehow.

"Yes," he replied, running a hand through his disheveled hair as he finally got to his feet. "It was bothering you that I was sleeping at the mill."

Hope sparked in my chest. Maybe he hadn't been with anyone else recently? Rastin's advice echoed in my mind:

you don't walk away from a man like Kicks. He was right, but I didn't see a way forward.

"Thanks," I said.

"I wanted to talk to you before Charlie got up. I know you were looking at the maps, and I can guess why."

This was no surprise. I'd left handwritten notes of possible places I could live and be self-sufficient on different pages. Most of the places were near small bodies of water, where fishing might be feasible. The maps had a layer of dust and seemed like they'd never been used. Who would imagine he'd suddenly want to look at them?

"I don't want to leave, but I can't shake the feeling that it might come to that," I said. I'd never wanted to lie about it. Part of me still hoped some miracle would occur that would allow me to make a home here with Charlie and, yes, Kicks.

"I reached out to the guide in California. He couldn't tell me much over the phone, but he said if we go there, he'd try to help, maybe give us an idea if it's you and there's something we can do to fix it. It's a long shot, but it's all we've got at the moment. I would've mentioned it earlier but there were a couple of hiccups."

Me. I was the hiccup. No one wanted anything to do with me—not even a pack thousands of miles away. No one but Kicks was standing by me, and yet in order to not ruin his life and Charlie's, I might have to leave them both.

"We'll work this out. Just promise me you won't take off on your own?"

"I'll try," I said, knowing it was the best I could offer. He deserved honesty. If I could say goodbye when the time came, I would, but I wouldn't make that promise.

———

Kicks had headed out, likely to the mill or to tackle another project in need of repair. The community had enlarged, and the growing pains were far from over. I'd grab a hammer and help if I didn't think it would scare away all the other workers.

I'd just dropped Charlie at school, which was going better than I'd hoped, when there was a knock at my door. An older man stood outside, looking in. They'd said Zetti was the oldest in the pack, but this man appeared to have some years on her. With so many people around, a stranger wouldn't have been easily let in. As I looked past him, no one seemed to notice or care about his presence.

"Can I help you?" I asked, opening the door.

"My name is Old Freddy. Wanted to pay my respects to the new mate." He had the kind of friendly demeanor of the lucky few who could put anyone at ease, even me.

"Oh. Um, okay. Would you like to come in?" I held the door open.

He walked in, leaning on his cane, looking about the place.

"Can I get you something to drink?" I offered, trying to be polite.

"Nah, I'm all good," he said, sitting on the couch as if he planned to stay a while. "Nice little home you have here."

"Thanks." I'd figure he would've been in here before, but maybe he didn't get out much?

"Lots of tongues wagging, but I can tell you're a good sort."

"Thank you. You might be in the minority, but I appreciate the support."

"I wouldn't upset yourself about Zetti. She wasn't as

good as they say she was. It's one of the reasons I wanted to come have this chat with you."

"Um, okay." This was not a conversation I'd been expecting, but when someone this old spoke to me, I liked to hear them out.

"She wasn't that good," he repeated, louder this time.

"I appreciate your trying to make me feel better, if that's what you're doing." It was really the only thing that made sense.

"I'm not trying to make you feel better. I'm telling you, Zetti wasn't that good. Never could prove it, and no one would take me seriously, but she was a bad apple. I knew her my entire life, longer than anyone here. She hated humans with every fiber of her being. I heard whispers that she killed some, too. Before she started putting on the act, she did a lot of things she shouldn't have. She wasn't the saint she's made out to be. If your gift worked on her, it was for a reason."

I nodded, not sure what to say. Part of me wanted to pump him for more details. Another part of me was afraid it was some kind of gag. Was the pack screwing with me now? Was this a practical joke?

I was relieved of having to say anything because Old Freddy suddenly got up, his eyes widening. "Oh no. She's coming for me. Best get going."

He made his way to the door, where a young woman appeared. "Old Freddy, are you telling your tales again? You know that's not nice."

"It's not tales if it's true," he said as he walked out of the house.

The young woman turned her attention to me. "He likes to sneak some sips and then gets creative. I wouldn't listen to him," she said, then moved to follow him.

She leaned closer to him as they walked away, whispering something I couldn't hear, but I would've sworn she was warning him not to visit me again.

———

Logs burned in the fireplace, casting a warm glow and the scent of wood through the room. The crackling was the only sound as I waited for Kicks to return home for the night. Charlie had gone to sleep hours ago.

He'd had to run out earlier because the repair to the mill hadn't held, but I knew I'd never be able to sleep until I got this off my chest.

The door finally opened and Kicks walked in. "I told you I'd sleep here. You didn't have to wait up for me."

"That's not it."

"What's wrong?" he asked softly as he settled on the couch.

"I had an unexpected talk with someone today," I said, curling my legs under me.

"Did someone give you a hard time?" he asked, the tendons in his neck immediately tensing. "Just so we're clear, I'm not Duncan. When someone comes at you, I want to know about it."

I didn't need the reminder of how different the two of them were. It was more obvious every day. When I first committed to coming here, I'd kept my distance, afraid I'd get hurt. The situation had completely flipped. Now I was afraid just being around me was hurting him.

"No, nothing like that," I replied, shaking my head. "I want to talk to you about it, but I don't want it to come off the wrong way."

"I won't judge. I'll just listen," he assured me.

I bit my lip, hesitant to repeat the conversation. If it was a gag, I'd look like a fool. I wasn't sure I believed Old Freddy's words. I swallowed hard, feeling like the sound echoed in the quiet room.

"I just want your honest opinion. I don't want you to take what I'm going to tell you as my trying to make excuses for what happened."

"Understood," he said.

"Someone told me today that Zetti wasn't always such a good person. He said she wasn't who she appeared to be. He said he knew her when she was younger, and she hated humans. He even suspected she'd murdered some. I don't want to buy into it too much. I'm afraid because it makes me feel better about what happened, and I'm clinging to it to justify that. And he might be making this up."

"And you think that maybe what he told you could explain what happened?" Kicks asked.

"I'm not trying to throw excuses out there. I wasn't looking for him to speak to me. I'm just telling you about his visit, and I was curious if you've ever heard something like this before."

"No, but she also didn't live here her whole life. She was originally from a pack in Northern California," he explained.

"Do you speak to them? Is there any way we could follow up on this?" I asked.

"If you want to find out this kind of information, it's better to go in person. Who told you all this?"

"Old Freddy. Do you think you could talk to him? See if you can sniff out a lie in his words?"

He froze and then leaned back. "You want me to talk to *Old Freddy*?"

"If you could. I didn't think it would be that big of a deal." At the mention of the name, his whole demeanor had seemed to shift.

"To *Old Freddy*?" he repeated, as if he hadn't already asked that.

"Yes, to Old Freddy," I said firmly.

He narrowed his eyes. "I don't think that's going to be something I can help you with."

"It's fine. I'll try again on my own."

He'd repeatedly said he wanted to help, and the first thing I asked for, he wouldn't do it. He stared at me as if he couldn't believe I'd even ask such a thing. Then he wondered why I didn't ask for help?

"Pips, it's not that I won't. I can't. It's—"

"It's fine. You don't need to explain." I got off the couch, and he stood at the same time, grabbing my arm before I could leave.

"Pips, Old Freddy is dead. He's been dead for a couple of decades."

"Dead?" I asked, my voice barely a whisper.

"Yes. *Dead.*"

I only managed to shape an O with my lips. Well, on the bright side, that was a very good reason he couldn't help. At least my faith was restored in Kicks, even if I'd just shown my hand more than I'd wanted to.

"Are you sure there isn't another Old Freddy?" I asked, grasping at straws.

"There was only ever one Old Freddy."

There was no way I was telling him he had a nurse of some sort with him. She must've been a ghost too. Or something...

What was I becoming? It seemed as if no matter what I

did, I was surrounded by death. I leaned a hip on the couch, trying to keep my composure and my legs underneath me. What I wouldn't give to go back to the good old days of wondering where my next meal was coming from.

"You don't look as shocked as I'd imagine," Kicks said, watching me closely, his hand still on my arm.

I moved back to the couch, missing the feel of his touch the second he let go.

"Because I might not be," I said. "After I transitioned, being able to kill people wasn't the only thing that changed. There are things that appear to me now. Well, not exactly things, but people." My voice trembled slightly. I hadn't seen Death in a while, and I wasn't ready to go there. The dead people were bad enough.

"You can speak to Jaysa," he said, his tone steady, as if he had already known, or at least strongly suspected it.

"You knew?" I asked.

"Remember when my pack member died throwing the ax at the hotel? That night you talked about Jaysa telling you things that you couldn't have known unless she'd spoken to you beyond the grave."

I remembered that night like I'd recorded it in hi-def in my mind. When he hadn't pushed me for more details, I'd thought I'd skated.

"You knew this whole time? Why didn't you say something?"

"It was a guess, and if you'd wanted to tell me, you would've." He walked closer. "Are there others?"

I wasn't sure if he wanted to know or felt compelled to ask.

"There's Widow Herbert, too."

"Anything else I should maybe know?" he asked, raising an eyebrow.

"I think we should just leave it at that for now," I said, not wanting to freak him out with anything else. This was plenty.

He nodded, looking satisfied to leave some things unsaid.

"I think we're going to have to get to California at some point soon," he said, finally breaking the silence after a couple heavy moments.

I nodded. I'd gladly go anywhere that offered answers at this point.

Chapter Fifteen

KICKS WAS SITTING on the couch in the middle of the afternoon. I tried not to stare, but there was something altogether odd about the whole situation. I glanced outside again and could see the rest of the pack going about their day, still building and working. Was he not feeling well and didn't want to tell me?

There was a soft knock at the door before Evangeline let herself in.

"Hey, came over to see if you want to get tea with me and the ladies?"

She had a smile fixed on her face like a bad actor who was trying to follow a script. It wasn't that Evangeline didn't smile, but not quite this wide or forced—or prolonged. It stank of a setup, even to my inferior nose.

"That sounds like a great idea. You should go. I'll be here when Charlie gets back from school," Kicks said.

I glared at him. "What are you two doing? Whispering in the corner on how to get me out of the house?"

Evangeline shot an accusing look at Kicks. "I told you it

was a stupid idea. That she wasn't just going to jump up and say, 'Yippee, let's go.'"

"The more you get out of the house and let them see you, the sooner they might get over it," Kicks said to me, ignoring Evangeline's glare.

"It's not going to work." I could feel the tension in the pack every time I was near. They wanted to run from me, and no one could blame them. Even if I hadn't killed Zetti, her death had something to do with me. We all knew it, even as some of us pretended it didn't.

"If it doesn't, we'll deal with it then, but at least try," Kicks replied.

Fine. Haunt them all with my presence until he came to terms with it. After he'd tried to bully them all into accepting me, I felt as if I owed him that. Plus, what if he was right? Maybe it could work? If it didn't, it would make it easier in the end, when I did have to leave, to prove I'd exhausted all possibilities. I still had no idea where I would go, if I should take Charlie with me or whether he'd be better off here. The idea of leaving him behind made me willing to try anything.

"Deal with it how?" Evangeline asked, losing that forced smile as her eyes ping-ponged between Kicks and me. "What does that mean? You two are talking about leaving?"

"We're not talking about leaving permanently," Kicks stated, as if he'd chiseled the words into granite.

That might've been technically true. He hadn't put that option on the table. I had. Either way, his words seemed to smooth out the worried lines on Evangeline's face as she nodded.

If I did go, I wasn't taking Kicks with me, no matter

what he thought. This was his home and I wouldn't take that from him. Plus, Charlie would need him.

Either way, it looked like I was going to tea.

"Do they know I'm coming?" I said, trying to draw her attention to a different topic.

"Not exactly. I hinted, but I thought it would be best to leave it vague. You know, until I was sure you'd come."

And so they didn't go running for the hills when they found out. Everyone would suddenly be backed up with work or not feeling so well if they knew I was coming. I'd probably be lucky if they didn't poison me.

"Let me go and get changed." I'd at least look good before they all ran from me.

My jeans weren't too shabby, but I put on nicer boots and a sweater that I'd gotten recently from the stash Evangeline gave me. It was enough to not be insulting to them, as if I'd made some sort of effort.

I walked back into the living room as Evangeline was nodding to Kicks and saying, "I'll make sure."

He'd clearly given her a list of instructions as to a curfew or babysitting detail. I wasn't sure which, and I was okay not knowing. It didn't matter anyway. He thought he was managing me with this situation, but in truth, I was managing him.

"Let's go." I stretched out as big a smile as I could paint on. It probably looked as fake as hers. "You have to do me a favor," I said to Evangeline. "Just to be on the safe side, don't touch me, okay?"

"To be honest, I wasn't really planning on it." She giggled. It was probably a nervous giggle, but it made me laugh as well, until we were both giggling.

I walked out of the cabin beside her and could feel my

hackles rising as soon as I did. People were watching me, probably wondering what I was doing out and about at this time of day. The only time they saw me was when I walked Charlie to school.

The only good thing about their giving me a wide berth was I could talk a little more freely.

"What was Kicks' previous mate like?" Of all the things I should've asked her about, like strategic questions about the terrain around here or how far to the main road if you walked... No, I asked about *this*.

Evangeline jerked her gaze to me. "Verity? Kicks mentioned her?"

"Not much. Just that she'd passed away. I was curious what she was like."

She nodded. "I don't know if I'm the most objective person to answer this because she was more than a pack mate to me. She was like a sister. I'm afraid I might paint too rosy a picture, but it's hard when the love runs deep."

"It's okay. Just speak your truth." I was afraid to hear it, even though I'd asked. This had been someone Kicks chose, and probably not for convenience or to make a transition easier. He'd chosen her for her, and I couldn't help but feel jealousy well up over a dead woman.

"She was like having a piece of sunshine in your life," Evangeline said. "Even when you were having a bad day, she'd come around and know just the right joke or thing to say. It was impossible to be down around her. Didn't matter what happened earlier. She'd brighten it up. She was a beautiful person, and it had nothing to do with how she looked, which isn't to say she wasn't pretty. She was, but that's not what drew people to her."

What had I expected to hear when I asked? That she had

been a miserable troll? That wasn't who Kicks would choose to spend his life with.

"How did she die? You shifters seem pretty hardy."

"It was sudden. No one saw it coming." She took a seat on a bench we were passing, sort of slumping as her eyes seemed to focus somewhere else. "Her and Kicks came down to my restaurant and had dinner with me two nights before she passed. We all laughed and had a great time. It was one of those nights you know you'll always remember. At the time I hadn't known it would be in a bittersweet way.

"At one point, when we were alone, she'd confided in me that her and Kicks were planning on starting a family. I got the impression that she might've preemptively started, if you know what I mean. I called her the next day to tell her she needed to come back soon. We'd had so much fun. She said she would but hung up pretty fast. She said she wanted to lie down because she was feeling a little under the weather. She was dead by that evening."

"I'm so sorry." I waited, hoping she'd say more but afraid to press.

"I'm not completely sure what happened, but I have a guess, not that I've ever gotten it confirmed or would even try, because I know that would just cause more pain."

She took a few breaths that seemed too heavy for her slight frame.

Her gaze flickered to the ground and then me, as if she were debating something. "There's a sickness that sets in with some shifters right after they get pregnant, like a day or so after the egg attaches to the womb, and it can kill them. We don't know exactly why, but it's hypothesized that the egg is incompatible with the mother. Pregnancy with shifters is different than with humans. A human female might miscarry, and shifters do miscarry, too. But sometimes the embryo, as small as it is, can kill the female shifter."

"Is that common?"

"No. It's not. It's more likely with a strong gene pool."

"By strong gene pool, you mean like an alpha?"

She nodded, knowing exactly what that was implying. "I wouldn't worry. You're human. The chance of your getting pregnant is almost zilch, and even if by some miracle you did, it wouldn't likely be a shifter embryo."

A picture was forming, and I wasn't sure if it helped me as much as Evangeline thought it would. "How long ago did she die?"

"Ten years. He's had his flings here and there, but nothing serious since then."

"What about Bri? He had a thing with her. That didn't head anywhere?" How could it not have? She was as nearly perfect a woman as I'd ever seen.

Evangeline was shaking her head before I finished. "He liked her, but that wasn't going anywhere. He kept his distance, and not just geographically, if you get my meaning."

Because he feared it had been partly his fault that Verity died. He hadn't mated with me just because of convenience, as I'd imagined. It went deeper than I'd known. The pack had probably wondered when he'd take a new mate, and how many of the female shifters hoped it would be them? When he mated with me to give the pack a guide, it gave him an excuse to mate with a human. He wouldn't have to worry about getting me pregnant when odds were I couldn't carry a shifter baby. I'd thought he hadn't cared that I was human. He'd wanted me *because* I was human. I was the easy way out, the safe way.

"Why do you look like that?" Evangeline asked.

"Like what?"

"Like I burned your toast."

"Oh no, it's just sad, is all." On more levels than I'd speak of. "Come on, I don't want to keep them waiting. They're already going to be cranky enough when they see me."

Chapter Sixteen

A COUPLE of women were looking through the window as we approached, their mouths gaping open. I wasn't sure if it was in shock or horror. Probably both. It was no more than I'd expected. They hadn't liked me that much the first time I showed up to this tea, and that was before Zetti died.

"They'll get past it," Evangeline said with a halfhearted smile as we got to the stoop. She opened the door and then held it open for me with her boot propped on the bottom, going above and beyond to make sure we didn't touch.

Evangeline, who sincerely liked me, was struggling to get over what happened. Why would people who hadn't known me get past it? I'd ignored the warning signs of overstaying my welcome, and I wasn't going to ignore them again. It was time to get serious about an exit plan.

"Ladies, look who decided to join us for tea and cake!" Evangeline called out.

Six faces met mine with different degrees of fake smiles. Some barely managed not to scowl, while some were mildly convincing. No one in this group would be winning an Oscar anytime soon.

I'd seen them all before. The only one who I'd had a strong dislike of was Louise, who of course was barely acknowledging me.

Evangeline poured us both some tea as we settled at the table. Louise, who happened to be closest to me, made a show of sliding her chair farther away.

"So, what's on everyone's agenda for the spring season?" asked Naomi, a younger lady who handled the laundry.

She avoided meeting my gaze when she spoke. She obviously didn't want to know what *my* spring plans were.

They began to chatter, talking about what they were planning on doing with crops, and other mindless chatter. I sipped tea, staring at the clock and wondering how long I'd have to sit here before I could make an excuse to leave. Evangeline shot me apologetic looks here and there.

"So what are your plans, Piper?" Louise asked. "I mean, do you have any?" She was openly condescending.

"*Louise*, you better watch your mouth," Evangeline said, eyeing her up like she was going to drag her out of the room in another minute.

"What? I'm just asking about her plans. I'm trying to be polite and inclusive."

"We all know—"

"It's fine," I said calmly. "I don't care much what she says or does. She couldn't get the man she wanted, and she's obviously bitter about it, but that's understandable."

"What? You think he really wanted *you*?" Louise got to her feet, if only to be able to look down upon me. "You're a mess, a monster, and a pariah. He has to threaten people to even get them to speak to you. Yeah, you're a *real* catch."

I stood. It was time for me to leave. Arguing or fighting with her wasn't the right move, and worse, her words hit home. Everything she said was true, and I knew it better than anyone.

Before I had a chance to leave, Louise dropped to the ground. It was like time stopped as we all stared at her form. She'd been healthy and laughing a second ago, and now she was gray and dead. It happened almost instantaneously.

Naomi let out a high-pitched scream. Everyone else ran from the building, and I just stood there. The only person left with me was Evangeline. She looked as frozen as I was. Finally her eyes lifted from Louise to me, and I could see her thoughts written as clear as day.

"Did you do that?" she asked. "I know she wasn't nice to you. I didn't like her either, but…"

She'd already decided I had done it, in spite of her question. She took a step back from me and shook her head.

"No. Or I didn't consciously… I don't know." Another person was dead. I hadn't touched her, not even a graze. I was too aware now to doubt that, especially with people I didn't like. My hands were shaking as my mind rebelled against what had happened. It was me. Somehow, I was behind these deaths. There was no other explanation.

Evangeline went to kneel beside the body but stopped short of touching her, as if whatever I'd done would spread.

Kicks burst into the room and then took a look at Louise on the ground, and then me.

"Where's Charlie?" I asked.

"I left him with Magnum as soon as I saw the commotion. What happened?"

"I—I don't know." I wasn't crying. I couldn't even really think straight as I began to shake.

"She didn't even touch her," Evangeline said. The words didn't sound like a defense of me, more shock that I killed so easily.

Buddie, Rastin, and Crackers filed into the room seconds later.

"Watch the door," Kicks said, and Buddie immediately took the lead.

"Holy shit. Another one?" Rastin said. "I mean, obviously you're not *trying* to kill them, because anyone who was wouldn't do it like this. They'd at least lure them into the woods or something. This…" He waved his hand at the body as he looked at me. "Seriously, you gotta get your shit together and get a handle on this crap. At least learn to be discreet."

It was too late for discretion. That ship had sailed.

I didn't know how to respond, and no one else did either. Rastin had basically laid out the way that probably most in this room felt. They thought I was a serial killer who couldn't get her act together. I was a blundering, messy, accidental serial killer who some of them happened to like. Or had.

I wasn't sure if Kicks was still going to insist things would be okay or accept reality, but I knew the truth of it, even as numb as I was. I had to leave. But now what? How did I get out of here? Would they rip me apart before I left? I shouldn't have waited so long. I'd known it wasn't going to work out, and now here I was, about to flee another pack.

"We need to get back to the cabin and figure this out," Kicks said.

There was no figuring anything out. There were no options left on the table but my fleeing.

"What about Louise?" Crackers said, pointing to the body.

Kicks looked at her for a second and said, "Carry her out the back and put her in the cold house. We'll figure out the rest later."

Chapter Seventeen

CHARLIE WAS at Magnum's cabin, which we could see from our cabin's window. I was sitting on the couch as Kicks, Rastin, Buddie, and Evangeline talked by the window. They'd been chatting in hushed tones for close to half an hour, as if they could decide my fate. Those days were over. I was deciding my own path.

"I can't stay," I said, interrupting their quiet chatter. "Not after this. It doesn't matter whether I'm causing the deaths or not. I have to leave."

"She's right. It's too much," Evangeline said to Kicks, then turned to me. "I'm sorry. I don't want that to be the case, but there's no point in denying it."

She looked almost as unsettled as me. It didn't matter what Kicks said. She knew this situation was beyond repair.

"Kicks, she's right," Rastin said. "Your pack is on the verge of anarchy." He, on the other hand, didn't seem rattled but a realist.

"We go see the guide in California. He might have some answers. If we can understand what's going on, I think we can fix it." Kicks watched me as he spoke, trying to gauge my reaction, searching for a hint of what might truly be going on in my head.

I didn't give him much more than a nod. Going to another guide wouldn't solve this problem. It would only buy me some time to figure out my next steps. I knew I had to get out of here.

But what about Charlie? I couldn't leave him here, not now. He might be safer far away from me, but after what had just happened? Would his relation to me still leave him untainted by my crimes? I couldn't drag him to the California pack, where I wasn't welcome. I didn't know what to do with him, but being with me wasn't the answer, not until I knew what I was doing, where I was going, and what I was becoming.

"Buddie, Rastin, I need you guys to do something for me. I know it's a lot, but I need this." I stood but didn't make the mistake of going closer.

"What is it? You know I've got your back," Buddie said.

"Of course we will," Rastin said.

"I want you to take Charlie to visit Maddocks' pack in Florida for a couple of weeks. I want him out of here."

"Definitely," Buddie said, nodding.

"I was about to run through the roster here anyway," Rastin said. "I wouldn't mind checking out Maddocks' lineup. Plus, who knew how damned cold it got here? I thought I was in the South. What's with this frigid weather?" He shuddered, trying to make a joke the way he always did when things were at their worst.

I couldn't laugh. Not tonight, knowing I had to leave and might never see these people again. Might never see Charlie.

"Take care of him? Please?" I said, trying to keep my

feelings from erupting and letting any of them know what my plans really were.

"Piper, you realize you're talking to a ride-or-die," Rastin said. "No one is touching a hair on that kid's head. You have my word. I'll die before anything happens to him, and I'm one tough son of a bitch to kill."

Kicks turned to Evangeline. "Can you handle things while we're gone? I'll ask Crackers to step up, too."

"You know I will," she said before taking a deep breath, as if the idea of Kicks' leaving was shredding her inside.

"Then we all leave tomorrow," Kicks said.

There were some hesitant glances back to me, as if they didn't know how to handle our goodbyes.

I nodded at them. "We'll all be back soon enough," I said, smiling as I lied.

"Guess we better go pack," Buddie said, walking toward the door with Evangeline.

Rastin paused, not following them out but staring at Kicks.

"I expect you to take care of her," he said. It was the first time I'd seen him speak to Kicks like this. "She's like a little sister to me, and I don't care what this looks like—she's good people."

"You don't need to tell me my business. She's *my* mate. No one will touch her," Kicks said.

Rastin stared at Kicks for a few seconds before he seemed to get whatever he needed from him. He nodded, and Kicks gave him a pat on the shoulder.

He looked back at me one last time. "It'll all be good," he said. "I will see you again."

I smiled as if I agreed. Nothing had been good before Death Day, and it had been getting worse ever since. I was done waiting for this *good* to happen. My bar for a good day was much lower. I was happy if no one died in my presence.

"We needed to go to California anyway." Kicks walked over and sat next to me. "We'll see what answers we get there."

"Why would you leave this? This is your home. It's where you belong." Belonging somewhere was so much more important than I'd ever given it credit for. I wouldn't take that away from anyone.

"I made a commitment, and I don't take that lightly. If you can't stay here, then we go together."

"I'm *relieving* you of your commitment." I wouldn't get into it again, but he owed me nothing. Less than nothing. I was in debt to him.

"I don't accept." His tone was firm.

I got up from the chair, feeling as if I had to put space between us. "Why can't you just let me go? Even if you wanted a guide, I'm not worth this aggravation. I'm not the guide that's going to bring your pack anything good."

He stood as well. "You're going to drag Charlie out of this pack, and then what? Roam alone, just the two of you? You think you're unkillable, but you're wrong. You'll never survive out there on your own."

"I'll be fine, and it's not your decision."

"Groza has a price on your head. The second you leave this pack, you're dead. Word will get out, and they'll come hunting you. I'm the only thing keeping you alive, and even that's iffy at this point."

It was even worse than I'd known. If I tried to take Charlie with me, I'd be guaranteeing his death.

This was why Kicks wouldn't let me leave. He didn't want *another* death on his hands.

I must've looked gray, because Kicks' tone softened as he said, "You didn't kill them. I *know* you didn't."

"Whether or not I killed them, they're dead, and the pack isn't going to feel any better about me in this lifetime."

"We will find an answer."

I doubted that, but I'd go with him to California and, if need be, disappear somewhere between here and there.

"I need to get some things in order so we can leave before morning." He stood there for a second before adding, "I'm going to have a couple of the guys keep an eye on the cabin while I wrap up a few details. If you see them, don't be alarmed."

I settled into the corner of the couch, pulling a throw tight around my shoulders as I realized the implication. The guards would be here to make sure I wasn't murdered.

"I'm not exactly helpless."

"It'll make me feel better."

I shrugged. I didn't care. It might be better if they were there. If Magnum brought Charlie back, I didn't want the kid's last memory of me to be a killing spree if someone tried to attack.

Chapter Eighteen

I LOOKED about the empty room.

"Widow Herbert?" I watched, waiting for her to appear. I hadn't seen her in forever, and I could really use her right now. She'd never stayed away this long.

"Jaysa?" I whispered, willing to take anyone who said they were on my side, even if they weren't alive or necessarily on the *right* side of things.

I pulled the blanket closer, trying to fight off the feeling of dark coldness that seemed to be taking root inside of me. Even if no one had died, there was something going wrong inside of me. I could feel it.

I got to my feet, pacing the cabin, calling out their names, hoping someone would appear. Maybe it was the cabin? Or this place? Was there something about this building and location that blocked them somehow?

Maybe if I got farther away from here?

There were three men, all with their backs to the cabin, standing out front.

I went to Charlie's room at the back of the house and

was relieved to see no one was guarding that area. The cabin was on the uppermost border of the community, without any structures behind it. It was highly unlikely anyone was going for a hike tonight, considering what had happened.

I opened the window, the sounds of the river hiding any noise of my departure.

I hiked up into the mountain, my steps hurried, knowing Kicks would come looking for me as soon as he found the cabin empty. He'd be the only one who would. No matter what the pack thought of me, no one else would have the balls to track me alone.

I pressed harder, pushing myself to hike as fast as I could. This had to be done alone. A conversation like this could not be overheard.

It wasn't more than fifteen or twenty minutes when I sensed something. There wasn't so much as a crinkle of leaves underfoot, but I wasn't alone. I spun fast, trying to spot her. I couldn't see Death, but I could feel her presence.

"I know you're here."

I waited. The feeling of *other* screamed out its presence to some inner sense I didn't used to possess. That small darkness I'd sensed within me felt like it was pulsing, as if it recognized the presence nearby, maybe even craved it. This feeling that had started after Zetti's death and grown since was *somehow* linked to *her*. That realization nearly drove me to my knees, making me want to heave, except I couldn't. Not with her around.

"Where are you? I know you can hear me. I need you to come out." I circled, waiting for Death to appear, knowing she would after she finished toying with me. "What do you want from me?" I was nearly screaming, and I didn't care who heard me anymore. My desperation had become palpable.

There was a chill in the air, a frost that was even colder than usual, hovering.

"Don't you know?" Death said.

I spun and there she was, not even five feet away, her head tilted at that unusual angle, staring with those completely black eyes that sent shivers through me. It was hard not to be alarmed by what her stare alone might do to my soul.

"No. I don't know. So why don't you tell me and we'll be done with this game you're playing?" Even speaking to her unsettled me in a way nothing else could. To ask questions of her stole the air from my lungs, but the idea of life continuing on this way was unfathomable to me.

She was smiling, walking closer and shifting the angle of her head in an odd way as she looked me over.

"You're an anomaly," she said. "You're not of my realm, but you aren't of this realm, either. I don't know where you belong. Maybe both. Maybe neither. You're like me but not. I can sense you even when I'm not near you, the way I can sense the other parts of me—but different."

I couldn't stand the riddles anymore. I needed answers only she could give, and I'd get them today. "Did I kill Zetti and Louise?"

"*I* killed them." She laughed.

"It was you? I didn't do this. I didn't just kill someone for no reason." This whole time, I'd been sick with terror. That it was me. That I'd become some kind of freak. I wanted to laugh, cry, scream. Every possible emotion was pumping through me. Even if it looked like I was the cause, their blood was not on my hands.

"Yes." She circled me, moving too smoothly to resemble anything remotely human.

"Why?" My joy was cut short as she smiled. It was like being doused by an arctic wave. I never wanted to see Death smile again, not like this, in her knowing way.

I'd dreaded her appearance since the moment I first sensed her, even though she'd even offered me favors in the past. Well, if that was how you categorized killing Groza. So why do this now? Why rip me apart mentally? Make me fear being near the people I loved? Kill those around me?

"Because I wanted them dead. They were a threat to you, and I've decided *I* need you."

"For what?"

"They need to know what they did, what's coming. They all need to know. They took something that wasn't theirs to take. They took what was *mine* and used it."

She was seething with rage so fierce the trees around us frosted over and the shadows grew darker, and then it was as if it were night. All sunlight perished and an arctic chill began spreading. A foreboding filled me, and I wasn't sure I dared ask the question—but how did I not?

"Do you mean…Death Day? They used something from you to cause Death Day?" I wasn't sure who *they* even were yet.

"*Yes.*" Her answer was like a clap of thunder, vibrating through me.

I didn't budge. I was afraid to breathe as she stared, her normally black eyes shining red.

"They took what wasn't theirs, and they will be punished. The people behind Death Day, the ones who purged the world of so many souls at once, stole from me, and I will get vengeance."

Even as the temperature dropped another ten degrees, I could feel the white-hot anger flowing from her.

"What does any of this have to do with me?"

"*I. Can't. You* will be my vengeance upon them." She stepped closer.

I backed away.

I didn't care about holding my ground, not with Death. There was no delusion of balance of power. She could take my life in a second, and I wouldn't have enough time to beg her to spare me before it was over.

"Why me? You don't need me. You're *you*. What would you need me for?" I continued to back away from her, but she kept following me.

"I don't only want them dead," she said. "I want them to know they're going to die and why. I want them to be waiting for it to come, to fear it, to dread it. I want them to pay with more than just their death. I want the fear to be so thick that they take their own lives to escape what's coming for them. I want them to pay so brutally that the story will be passed down for a millennium."

"Then do it." I didn't even blame her. I harbored as much hate for these people as she did. But I still didn't understand why she was telling me all this. Why did she need me?

"*I. Can't,*" she said, and her voice felt like it shook the ground underneath me. "There is a veil that hangs between what I am and what they can see. I need someone from this world, a vessel to carry out my deeds and allow me to flow through them."

She wanted me to be her monster. If I could've, I might've died from dread right then and there, but she'd probably force me to stay alive somehow.

"You will be untouchable. I'll teach you to be even more than you thought capable," she said.

"What if I don't want that?" Even if any of this sounded desirable, which it didn't, I'd learned one thing: magic had a price. You didn't change and only get the upside. There was no way what she was planning wouldn't cause a change in me. Maybe already had? "Are you that dark, cold feeling that's growing inside of me?"

"You should be happy if part of what I am transfers to you. Grateful for the power that it instills in you."

I didn't care what power that darkness inside brought. I didn't want it. It felt like a disease trying to take hold of my soul. If this kept happening, *I'd* wish for death.

"No. I don't want this. I won't do it."

"You must. You are the only one who can."

"Take some other person. Use someone that wants what you are offering. I don't." I could already kill with a touch. What would become of me after she channeled her magic through me? No. The mere thought of it made me stiffen, nearly strangled me with fear.

"There is no other. You *will* do this. Not only will you do this, you will *beg* me to do this." She spoke as if she knew what the future held. Whatever she knew, I hoped it didn't come to pass, because this wasn't what I wanted.

She was gone. The rough bark of a tree scraped at my back and my legs could no longer keep me up. I was nearly hyperventilating, my face wet with tears, sitting in the mud under the tree when Kicks found me.

He knelt in front of me, running his hands over my legs and then arms. "Pips, are you hurt?" He put his hand under my chin, lifting my face. "Pips? What happened? Did someone chase you here?"

"I'm okay. Nobody is here." There was only one silver lining—I might kill when threatened, but I wasn't the indiscriminate killing machine I'd feared. I wasn't *that* much of a monster. Not yet, anyway.

"What happened?" He scanned the perimeter and the ground, looking for tracks, trying to piece the scene together.

Death was gone from sight, but I still couldn't bring myself to say anything. I didn't know if I could. How did you tell someone that Death wanted you to be its vengeance? To use you to kill people and leave traces of whatever she was behind, inside of you? Planned on doing it again and again until you weren't even you anymore? How did you tell someone that?

He carried me back to the cabin, continuously looking around, trying to piece together what had happened.

He placed me in the chair and then pulled it closer to the fire.

"You have to tell me what happened. And don't say nothing. I can smell the fear on you, and your hands are trembling."

I stared at him kneeling in front of me and choked on the truth. Imagined the disgust on his face if he knew. I had to leave him anyway. I didn't want him to remember me as a monster. Instead of telling him, I looked down at my lap.

"I never wanted to force you to tell me anything. I wanted you to trust me, and to tell me things that bothered you because you wanted to. But no matter what I do, I can't earn your trust. I'll have to accept that. " He stood. "Make sure you pack light."

He walked away.

"It's not like that. I *do* trust you," I said to his back.

"This is trust?"

It was like my muscles were seizing around me, causing me to feel like my heart was being held in a death grip.

"Then let me leave on my own tomorrow." There was no point in his coming with me. There was no future for us.

He turned his head slightly, only his profile visible as he said, "I don't know why, but I can't seem to let you go to your death, even if I should walk away."

Chapter Nineteen

IT WAS PREDAWN when Buddie and Rastin appeared at the cabin to pick up Charlie. I'd woken him this morning to tell him about the trip, feeling as if I were about to retch the entire time. As sick as it made me, he'd been bouncing around since he heard. He'd wanted to go to a big amusement park since before Death Day. It wasn't going to be exactly the way it used to be, but he wouldn't know.

He ran toward the door, where the guys were waiting. I chased after him with a bag of cookies.

"Don't eat them all at once." I tucked them in his backpack as I plastered on my fake happy face. I refused to let him see me cry. I'd figure out some solution to all of this and be back for him. The idea of leaving him completely was too much to bear. There had to be a way.

"Piper, it's okay. You'll get to come next time," he said, then wrapped his arms around my waist.

I'd told him I had to stay behind this trip to help Kicks.

"I know," I said.

I tried to fake it a little better until he left. I watched as he skipped along toward the bikes, hating that he wasn't at least going in an ATV. I wasn't exactly in a place to dictate, so instead I waved from the door and watched them drive away.

"You ready?" Kicks asked as I turned back into the cabin.

Now that they were gone, I stopped acting altogether. It was hard enough to breathe past the tension between Kicks and me, let alone pretend to be happy.

I nodded. He grabbed both of our bags that had been stashed out of sight in the bedroom. As soon as the sounds of the guys' departure died down, we headed out.

Evangeline and Crackers met us over by the bike.

"Don't worry. We'll take care of everything here," Evangeline said, the lines across her forehead looked as if she were doing enough worrying for everyone.

"We got it covered," Crackers said, nodding to Kicks and then trying to give me a smile. "Good luck."

"Yeah, good luck," Evangeline added.

"Thanks," I said.

We got on Kicks' bike, heading out in search of answers. Yet nothing about it felt hopeful. Instead it felt like the beginning of the end. How could there be an answer to the problem I had? Death wanted to use me as her instrument.

We stopped several times through the first day of the ride, and I was happy for the lack of breaks. When we were riding, I didn't have to talk, or pretend or lie. I could just be and think about what was coming. I'd thought I could leave Charlie, but not after this morning. I'd have to figure something out. If there was no way of getting away from Death, I'd at least negotiate. I'd figure out a way to stay close to him. He'd lost too much already, and I wasn't leaving him if there were any other options. I just had to figure out how to make that happen.

A human pack was out of the question. As soon as he started to shift, he'd need guidance I couldn't give, and humans would kill him. Maddocks' pack, maybe? If they hadn't heard anything too horrible? Or could I stay nearby, farther up on the mountain here? Still be in his life but removed slightly? There had to be a way.

I still hadn't come up with any better options when Kicks pulled up to a small bungalow situated along a stream. There were a couple lounge chairs on a deck overlooking the view. It would've been a cute little weekend rental back when there were enough people to do that sort of thing.

I got off the bike, happy to stretch out my legs for a while and look around.

"You knew this was here?" His course had seemed too planned out for us to have ended up here accidentally.

"Yes. Several of us have used it before when traveling."

I took a few steps toward the door.

"Let me go first," he said, cutting in front of me.

I'd thought he wanted to make sure the place was empty, but instead he knelt, undoing some sort of booby traps.

He straightened and then held the door open for me to go in. It looked well kept too, if not updated in a good half-century. It was cozy, with the stone fireplace that drew you over. I ran a hand along the mantel.

"I wouldn't risk lighting a fire unless you're in the mood to kill something tonight," Kicks said.

It was a flippant remark, a quick statement he hadn't given much thought. And yet it burned. How could anyone get past my victim list at this point? I thought about it constantly, and obviously so did he.

"I'd rather be cold," I said, not going as far as defending myself but laying it out there all the same.

He froze and locked eyes with me. "I didn't mean it like that." His voice held a hint of regret.

"I know." He might not have meant it the way it sounded, but it was in his head. It was hard to fault someone when you were thinking the same thing.

"You can take the bedroom. I'll take the couch."

I peeked around the corner, only seeing one bed.

"Try to get some rest tonight. We've got to make a stop tomorrow."

"Where?" It was the first I'd heard of any detours.

"There's a small human community that acts as a trading post of sorts. It's a bit more than halfway between here and the California pack. It's good for information and to keep an eye on what's happening farther out from our borders. It keeps me plugged in."

"Who do *they* think you are, exactly?" It sure wasn't going to be the truth, not that I was judging. I was learning how the truth didn't always set you free in the hardest way possible.

There was a lengthy pause before he said, "A rancher."

I stared at him, trying to envision him with fresh eyes. Had I ever been naïve enough to see him as a rancher? No. My mother had once told me I'd come out of the womb with a cynical eye. I'd had a few slip-ups through the years, more lately than ever before. But not even my youngest of selves would ever see Kicks as a rancher.

"So you're happy-go-lucky traveling rancher Kicks?" It was hard not to laugh at the whole thing.

"Actually, it's Rancher Ed, who has a sister in California

I go and check on." A hint of a smile was forming on his lips. He couldn't even take this disguise seriously.

"Rancher Ed?" I wasn't sure these people had any information worth listening to if they believed *that* story.

"Yes. I'm going to go hunt us up some dinner. I'll be back in a few. Don't wander."

"Okay, *Rancher Ed.*"

He raised a brow.

"What?" I shrugged. "I'm practicing."

"You sound like a bad actor trying to talk with a twang," he said, smirking.

"That's why I have to practice, *Rancher Ed*," I said, laying it on even thicker.

It was the first lighthearted talk we'd had all day, and it felt nice to cut the tension for a second.

He laughed softly before he left.

Chapter Twenty

WE PULLED down a winding road the next morning, driving under a large ranch sign that brought back memories. It was just like an old TV series my mother had liked to watch when she was sick: *Dallas*. She'd watched it growing up, and toward the end of her life, when she couldn't seem to do much more than lie in bed, we'd binge-watched it together.

I wondered what she'd think of this place. It was like it was plucked right out of her show. There were horses and cows in the distance. They'd definitely had a good running start when the end of the world came.

There were a few men on the porch, drinking and talking to each other as we parked the bike. Some more people were out in the field, looking as if they were trying to get the animals settled in for the night.

Kicks nodded to the men on the porch as we walked up. They nodded in return, their eyes shooting to his possessive hand at the small of my back.

A blonde wearing a cocktail dress that would've fit right

in on *Dallas* was lighting candles and oil lamps in the grand hall. She turned and immediately smiled, but her eyes barely passed over me. The sound of her heels was dulled by the thick runner.

"Ed, I was wondering when I'd be seeing you again. It's been a minute." The way she smiled, the way she touched his arm, it appeared there was some history here as well.

How much history did he have? I'd thought maybe a novella, then a full-length novel, and now I was worried it was a series, and one that didn't end.

She'd still barely glanced at me.

"This is my wife, Julie," he said. "Julie, this is Blondie."

When was she going to move that hand? Did she not see his on my back?

"Hello." I watched her hand, waiting, wanting to wrench it off him.

I curved my arm around his waist like it belonged there. I figured if I hadn't killed him by holding on to his waist the entire time here, it was probably safe enough.

"Wife, huh?" She narrowed her eyes.

Oops. Looks like someone felt out of the loop.

"Recent development," he said. Kicks rubbed my back, and I tried not to melt. It was like my body was attuned to every touch of his.

"You're one lucky lady." Blondie finally moved her hand. There was a split second of silence before she shifted topics. "This is particularly good timing. Those guys who are getting that oil field up and running are here. They ran out, but they'll be back. If you can hang around, I can prob-ably arrange a sit-down with them in the morning?"

"That sounds great. Appreciated," Kicks said.

"Since you've got the missus with you this time, I'm

figuring you'll be wanting the blue room?" She glanced at me briefly, as if to see if I'd picked up on the hint.

How could I not? He'd obviously slept in her room, and her bed, last time. And *this time*?

"I'm sure it's perfect," I said before Kicks replied. There was only going to be one girl on the cover of this novel, at least until I decided what I was doing. If he had to mess around, it was not going to be with her, or in front of my face like this. No way.

Blondie still had a smile on her face, but her eyes were hard when they met mine. "You missed dinner, but I can fix you a tray of some meat and cheese. I'll run it up in a few."

Our bags in hand, he headed up the stairs.

"This way, my little wifey," Kicks said, a wide smile on his lips.

I grabbed my bag from him and tossed it on the bed as soon as we got into the room. "Did Bri know about your situation with Blondie downstairs? She *looks* like a Blondie, by the way."

"Is that why you're all worked up? Did you feel offended for Bri?" I wasn't looking at him, but I didn't need to. I could hear the smile in his words.

"How many are there? Is there going to be a new one in California, too? How many other places did you *visit*? You seem to like to *visit* quite a lot. Bri at least made sense. That one is a viper."

"It happened. I'm not a monk."

He looked like a man who wasn't used to going without for long, either. The idea that he'd lain with Blondie, had a connection with her that he'd never had with me, made me want to scream, punch him, and punch her as well, in no particular order.

"So who've you been sleeping with since you took me as your mate, since you can't seem to be celibate?" I was digging around in my bag, and I couldn't remember what I'd been looking for. My brain was short-circuiting, unable to get the image of him and Blondie out of my head. And I'd believed that mill story. Sure. I was going to have to ask Death if he'd been messing around with Louise. If Death was going to ruin my life, I better start getting something out of this deal.

"I haven't slept with anyone." He was close behind me, and then a hand grazed my hip, slid up to my waist, and then pulled me back against him. "You know, if you're going to start getting possessive, I'm going to start getting ideas."

"Like what? That I don't like to be embarrassed?" I sounded flustered. As soon as he touched me, it was as if I immediately became a big ninny.

"Embarrassed? Is that what it's called now? Looked more like jealousy to me, but what do I know—this is all business, right?" He pulled me closer, until my curves were forming to him.

"Yes. That's right," I said, but made no motion to pull away.

He dipped his head lower, his jaw brushing my temple. "You're sure that's what you want? A pure business relationship?"

He brushed my hair away from my neck, and his lips grazed the soft, sensitive skin of my neck.

He lifted his head right before there was a knock at the door.

"Ed?" Blondie called from the other side. It was all I needed to snap my sanity back into place. I shifted away from him until I was on the other side of the bed.

Kicks stared at me, shook his head as if he knew the moment was lost, and then opened the door.

Blondie was there with a tray of food. "Those guys said they'd talk to you at breakfast if you're interested."

"Sounds good. Thanks," Kicks said.

"Let me know if you need anything else," she said, smiling just for him.

"This should be it. Thanks again," Kicks said.

I was barely able to wait until he shut the door before I said, "You leave this room tonight and I'll gut you in your sleep."

He laughed. "You know, you're very territorial for my little human business partner."

I glared at him.

He was laughing again as he said, "I'll take the floor."

Chapter Twenty-One

THIS WAS my first trading negotiation since the end of the world, and I was feeling a little—jittery? Excited? Even though I wouldn't be doing much in terms of negotiating myself, it was a fun distraction from the current bleakness of my situation.

"They're waiting for you there." Blondie pointed to the side room. She was all smiles and roasted coffee as she watched us walk down the stairs. She handed us both coffees. Kicks took his. I took mine but with no intention of drinking it. She was a little too happy today for my comfort. "Everyone else is gone at the moment, so you can negotiate in private. I'll introduce you."

She led the way into the side room, and there was no way her hips naturally swung that much. If she swayed any more, she'd go topside. Kicks' eyes were focused over her shoulder and not somewhere south. Mine should've been focused on the two men in the room as well. They both had lean, hard looks to them, but that was probably true of most of the people left today, or at least the ones thriving.

"This is Ed and Julie." Blondie waved a hand to the two men sitting at the table. "Rex and Trigger."

Rex, the one with the shaved head and black goatee, eyed me up and down the second Kicks turned his attention to Blondie. That look was enough to double the amount of bile I had already, just from looking at these two. They reminded me of what I'd left behind in the apartment complex back in New York, maybe worse. They might've been a few miles farther down the road toward damnation. Didn't really matter, as I'd probably never see them again.

The other thing I had to keep remembering was that I wasn't as vulnerable as people seemed to think, or I kept thinking myself. I killed with a touch. The people I didn't kill, Death killed for me. My biggest problem was keeping people alive. I was turning into some sort of accidental Jacklyn the Ripper. Talk about churning up the bile.

Kicks pulled out a chair for me to sit. It wasn't as if he'd never done something like that before, but this seemed more calculated. He was demonstrating some significance in our relationship, placing an unspoken value upon me.

I didn't mind, considering if either of these two stepped out of line, I might add a couple to my body count. I'd like to try to get through a week without killing anyone, if at all possible.

"Heard you want to make a deal?" Rex said, his gaze flickering to me on the last word. "We'd be interested, depending on what you have to trade."

This guy left a sour taste in my mouth. It didn't bode well for the week's target of zero deaths.

"I'm a rancher and I hunt. I also have a lot of connec-tions. What were you in need of?" Kicks said.

Had he missed that signal of Rex's? He didn't miss

much. He *was* happy Rancher Ed today—maybe he wanted to play stupid.

"We'd be willing to trade for some grains and meat," Rex said.

Really? Was I becoming so cynical that I'd read these people so wrong? I relaxed in my chair. I still got an off feeling about them, but maybe they weren't that bad.

"I'm sure we can come up with an amount that will work for both of us," Kicks said.

Rex nodded. "One other thing." He waved his hand toward me. "We want her."

I groaned. Why did people so often meet my low expectations? Just when I'd had a glimmer of hope for their souls, they had to prove themselves the lowest of the low.

I glanced around the room, hoping Death wasn't lurking nearby. There was no reason to kill them just yet, even though they were gross human beings.

"She's not available," Kicks said, his voice shifting lower, like when he was ready to kill someone. He wasn't moving at all, like he didn't trust what would happen if he even allowed himself to flinch. I wasn't sure if he was breathing as he stared them down.

If I could've, I'd have explained this was a dead end and put a stop to it all. Rex had no idea what he was getting into. He thought he was wading around in a baby pool, but it was shark-infested waters. Neither of us were showing our teeth, but he was no competition for the people he was sitting across from, especially me. My own personal bodyguard was even worse than Kicks. She didn't mess around when it came to threats.

"You can have her back. We just want to borrow her for a while." Rex smiled, and his friend laughed.

Six months ago, this would've terrified me. Not now. I couldn't quite even get upset enough to care. Unfortunately, Kicks wasn't feeling the same. He was going to explode where he sat, and these two idiots didn't realize they'd lit the fuse on an atomic bomb.

"She's. My. Wife." His words were coming out through a clenched jaw. I had to give it to Kicks—if you were with him, he protected you to the death. He wouldn't just wage war for you. He'd wage a grudge match that would go on for a thousand years.

"It's our gasoline that you and your settlement are going to need. Are you saying one woman is more valuable than gas?" Rex said.

"Yes." Kicks got to his feet and pulled me up with him, as if he thought I'd linger behind with these two.

Rex and Trigger got to their feet, too.

"We can either make a deal that will work for all of us or we can do it a different way," Rex said.

"If you're smart, you won't speak another word," Kicks said.

I put a hand on his arm. I wasn't looking to get traded for some gas, but I wasn't ready for him to show his true colors in this place. He could stand firm and yet not kill them.

"Can we talk outside for a second?" I asked.

Even though the rage wasn't directed at me, the look in Kicks' eyes was still a little overwhelming. How stupid were these men to assume they had the upper hand?

"Please?" I said.

I could see Kicks begin to bend, turning slightly toward the door. The tension was still high, but there was a slight chance of turning this around if I could manage to get him out the door and talk to him alone. Who cared how horrible these people were? What they said?

"That's right. Listen to the wifey. She obviously doesn't mind the idea." It was the first time Trigger had spoken, and I wished he hadn't.

Kicks froze. Dumbass Trigger just *had* to say something. He couldn't let me get out the door and save his sorry hide.

"It doesn't matter what they say," I said, stepping in front of Kicks, in between them and him.

"Now she's going to try to protect him from getting into a fight he can't finish. Knew she was the smarter one," Rex said, and the two of them laughed.

"Piper, you need to step out of the way," Kicks said.

"I think—"

He picked me up and placed me behind him.

"Look, we tried to do it nicely, but we're taking your woman whether you want us to or not," Rex said. "Now you won't get anything out of the deal. There's not enough women left. She's the most valuable thing you have. Did you really think you could keep her on your farm?"

Two more armed men appeared in the doorway to the sitting room. Blondie ducked back behind the door, but not before I saw her in the hall behind them, not even a little surprise on her face.

"Tell your men to back off before I have to kill you all," Kicks said.

There was no way we were getting out of here now without someone dying, and it wouldn't be us. So which was worse? Did I try to stay out of the fray and let Kicks shift and kill them? Could he kill four at one? Or would I have to step in, have them all drop and convulse while turning an ugly shade of gray? If I killed, would that horrible feeling of something *other* inside me grow? That was the scariest thing of it all.

"It's over," Rex declared. "Walk away nicely and we'll let you live. Otherwise we'll kill you in front of her."

"The only ones who're going to die are you and your friends," Kicks said. He sounded pretty confident. Maybe no gray men today?

He shifted, positioning me in the corner of the room behind him.

"Stay there," he said, his voice roughened to where I had to strain to understand. He was about to shift.

He was going to take on all these men alone. I'd seen the creatures he and his pack shifted into. They weren't like big, furry dogs. They were the stuff of horror movies. If someone had ever dreamt them up and put them on the big screen, it would be an instant R rating. He could handle this. And if he couldn't, I'd step in—or Death would. For now, I was going to let him take his shot. I'd do pretty much anything to avoid having that feeling inside me grow.

A low growl filled the room. I'd been up front at a concert once, near a speaker where the bass felt like it vibrated through you. You didn't so much hear the noise as feel it.

That's what this was like. They'd picked a fight they couldn't win.

There was a flash of fear on a couple of the faces, but Rex and Trigger didn't heed the warning, or think there was any way one man could fight them off. It was like they'd disregarded Death Day and what that meant altogether. This wasn't the good old days, where you could size up your opponent. There were things, *creatures* like Kicks and people like myself, who'd risen out of the shadows. Death

Day had been a line of demarcation, from what the world had seemed to be and the reality of what really existed. It looked as if they hadn't learned that lesson, but they were about to in the most violent of ways.

It wasn't until I heard the booming steps that signaled Death's imminent arrival that I knew for sure I wasn't going to be the one to kill them, or at least not all of them. For some reason, my killings didn't happen that way, as if maybe they were unnatural and untimed.

There wasn't any time to ponder it now, as Trigger moved in first, swinging wildly. Kicks swung back. Before he even completed the motion, his clothes had been shredded off him, and he gained a foot and a half in height, another foot in width, and was all sinewy muscle, claws, and fangs.

I nearly fell on my ass. I would've if the wall hadn't popped up behind me.

Trigger hit the ground, blood spraying out of his neck. The other three were no longer taking chances but coming at Kicks all at once, Rex with a chair in his hand and the other two with guns out.

The bullets bounced off his skin, landing on the ground. Kicks was literally bulletproof?

The rest happened too quickly to track. It was a blur of motion, with thumps as bodies hit the floor until there was silence.

Kicks had said the way I killed was no worse than what he did. I'd thought he was trying to be kind. He wasn't. It might've been worse.

I had trouble breathing. All I could see was blood and guts and a savagery that was, in a way, worse than Death Day. I was surrounded by an utter bloodbath.

One had his gut ripped open. Another had the veins and tendons hanging out of his neck, like spaghetti splayed on the floor.

Kicks, still in beast form, groaned and then slowly shifted back into human form.

"Go get the bags upstairs," he said. He cracked his neck, turning it this way and that and looking stiff in his skin.

I nodded, heading toward the hall and happy to be away from the wreckage. The only positive right now was still being on track for zero kills myself. I'd have to take the wins where I could.

I caught sight of Blondie ducking into a room on my way upstairs. I shoved the door open, and she jumped back.

"You knew what they were going to do. That's why the place was empty for breakfast." I didn't expect her to admit it, but I wasn't leaving here letting her think she'd gotten one over on us. I was too pissed for that.

"I didn't," she said, quite predictably. She was cute enough that she could probably manipulate plenty of the men who came here. I wasn't looking to fuck her, so it wouldn't work out as well.

She backed as far away from me as she could, probably thinking I could shift and kill her at any moment. I didn't have to shift. If I wanted her dead, she'd get no warning.

I *should* kill her. Left here alive, she'd talk. She'd tell stories of the monster. There were more humans than shifters. To think they weren't a threat would be as foolish as what they'd done downstairs, and we'd seen how that turned out. I wouldn't kill her because I feared that piece of darkness within me worse, but she needed a scare so she didn't talk.

I closed in on her, not stopping until her back was pressed against the wall and she was breathing rapidly.

"You say anything of this to anyone, and we will hear. Then we will come back and kill you. Do you understand?"

She nodded, a few tears escaping.

"I don't like you, but I'm allowing you to live because I'm giving you the benefit of the doubt that you didn't mean for this to happen. You speak, and I'll know that assumption was wrong."

She began to cry, and I didn't care. She'd tried to kill me, and I was losing the capacity for empathy for my enemies. I wasn't sure if this was life wearing me down or that insidious darkness I could feel infringing on my psyche. What was more terrifying was I *liked* that I didn't care. Those might be the only things that were saving her today. Right or wrong, she'd continue to breathe because of my own sense of self-preservation.

I turned my back to her, making sure she knew she was no threat to me. I hadn't made it out the door when there was the sound of yet another body hitting the ground.

I stopped, sighing, refusing to turn around and see her dead. I went to the other bedroom and grabbed our bags.

Death was waiting for me there.

"Why didn't *you* kill her?" Death said, glaring at me.

"Because I didn't *want* her dead. Why did you?"

"She betrayed you and would've caused a threat to you and the pack. You don't leave people like that alive."

Now she was worried about the pack? She'd just killed two of them off. I wasn't discussing it, not right now. We had to get out of here before anyone returned and the death toll grew.

I grabbed our bags, trying to ignore her presence.

Kicks stood at the bottom of the stairs, shirtless but with pants that were only slightly torn and blood-splattered.

The blood didn't bother me. It was as if I were becoming numb to the remnants of death, especially if I hadn't caused it.

What I wasn't used to was being near Kicks after he'd shifted. There was an intrinsic feeling of unpredictability as the energy coursed off him and seemed to squeeze out all the air in the room until all you could sense, breathe, feel, was him.

He tilted his head toward the door, and I nodded. He walked out, not asking what had happened upstairs, even though he must have heard the thump of Blondie hitting the floor.

He headed toward the bike that was parked out front. I got on behind him, and for once, there was no fear that I'd take him out. Right now, it felt as if he were indestructible.

I wrapped my arms around him, taking the excuse to hold on a little tighter than needed. Was this what life would be now?

Chapter Twenty-Two

KICKS DROVE the bike off the road, stopping in the middle of nowhere. We both got off, neither of us speaking as he unpacked his bag from the back and tossed it on the ground.

Were we stopping here for the night? It looked that way, but I was too raw, the feeling of darkness nagging at me, to ask him with the way his energy felt. I was afraid I'd be the spark to his bomb, or maybe vice versa. I wasn't sure who would blow first.

Kicks walked over to the edge of the woods and then stopped, his back to me. "Don't ever get in between me and the enemy," he said, his voice low.

"I was *trying* to help." I was too raw to have this argument, but it was unavoidable.

He turned to face me, his eyes burning. "I know exactly what you were doing, but they could've hurt you."

"I was trying to stop it from escalating. I was trying to salvage the situation before it went exactly as it did," I shot back, all the tension I'd had bottled up set to explode.

"There was no salvaging that situation." He spoke like it was an absolute, his jaw set.

"We don't know that."

"I know you shouldn't have put yourself in between me and them. That's not the world we live in anymore. You can't be that reckless," he said, his voice rising and the distance closing between us.

"I'm not some helpless little girl. I can kill with a touch. They. Weren't. Taking. Me," I said.

"You have no control over what you're doing. What if it didn't work?" he said.

He was so close I had to arch my neck back. "I was *fine*. Their hurting me wasn't a problem, but you wouldn't even listen."

"If you want a man that's going to sit back when you're threatened, that's not me. You knew who I was when you mated me," he said.

"And you know who I am. Not exactly helpless," I replied. I wouldn't even talk about how I'd been waiting to jump into the fray if he needed me.

Our gazes burned into each other's, the tension between us thick and palpable. My eyes slipped downward, to his mouth. I forced them back up, but it was too late. He could feel the attraction, see it in my eyes.

Before I could step back, his arms wrapped around me. His lips found mine. Instead of wanting to push away, I wanted to sink into him even more. His kiss obliterated my consciousness, overwhelming me with the raw emotions neither of us could put into words. It was as if all the tension, the fear, the anger collided in this one moment. I wanted to stay this way, to forget what had just happened and let the moment sweep me away.

His hands moved to my waist, pulling me closer as I tangled my fingers in his hair, grabbing on to him. Every brush of his lips, the feel of his tongue over mine, made me grab on tighter, arch into him.

And then I could feel the darkness pulsing to life within me. *It* wanted this. *It* liked this.

"I can't." I pushed at his chest until he dropped his arms.

"Why? You want this." His voice was ragged.

"You *know* why." Or mostly.

"I'm willing to take the risk."

"I'm not." It was as much as I could explain, because I couldn't tell him that I was corrupted, that there was something unclean in me, this darkness growing that was too much to bear. I'd rather have him think I was overreacting, which, given the circumstances, no one in their right mind would say. The reminder of how *it* throbbed at the connection with him pushed all desire from me.

He walked off into the woods. He didn't come back right away either, and the minutes piled up into hours. If he hadn't left the bike, I'd wonder if he was coming back at all.

I followed the sounds to the nearest stream, cleaned myself off, and then started a fire. I didn't care if the smoke signaled my location to others. The way I was feeling right now, I'd welcome someone coming to find me.

I didn't care anymore. The darkness felt like it was growing inside me, trying to encroach further.

I sat as close to the fire as I could, letting the heat seep into my bones. I focused only on good memories, on playing games with Charlie, talking with Widow Herbert, going to the park with my mother when I was little. I pulled up every good thought until the cold feeling was pushed away, more manageable. Until I felt more of myself again.

I looked up into the darkening sky.

"Widow Herbert?" I waited a few seconds and repeated her name.

I put my head in my hands, closing my eyes.

A chill filled the air and the darkness inside me thrummed to life again, trying to expand.

When I lifted my head, Death was standing there, looking at me.

It wasn't a coincidence that Jaysa and Widow Herbert had disappeared as Death had decided she had a use for me. It was her fault. I could feel it in my bones, in the coldness that was seeping into my core. This darkness in me was driving them away, or she was blocking them somehow.

"You got rid of them." I didn't soften the accusation. I was beyond caring right now.

"*We* don't need them."

We. She was calling us a *we* now.

"*I* need them." It helped somehow, especially Widow Herbert's comforting presence. Sometimes I felt like she was all I had to cling to these days when everything seemed to be falling apart. It felt like life had been black and white before Death Day, and now I was living a kaleidoscope that wouldn't stop shifting and changing.

"You don't," Death said.

I wanted to argue with her, but what was the point? She would do as she wanted. She could kill in a second with no remorse. She could steal every loved one I had left. She was the power behind Death Day, and that could never be forgotten.

She walked closer. "I need you, and you need me. No one else matters."

I didn't respond, staring into the fire and trying to ignore her.

She came closer. "Why didn't you let us have him? I *liked* that."

"You can feel what I feel?" I asked, stunned.

"I *liked* it." Her body seemed like it was vibrating. It didn't last long, but it was enough to sour my stomach.

The thought of her there, with us in some way, was nauseating. Somehow a part of our connection. Nothing was sacred anymore. I couldn't have a moment to myself or a moment with him. It was as if she owned a part of me I couldn't lose.

"You'll never have him," I said, not caring what the repercussions were.

"We shall see," she replied. She smiled, as if making me a promise, before disappearing.

———

I was still in the same spot when Kicks finally came back. I doubted he'd gone far. He wouldn't have been out of earshot, or at least I didn't think.

His flesh was clean, his hair wet. The stream had to have been freezing, but the cold never did bother him, not like me.

The other difference in him was immediately obvious. All the sharp edges were smoothed out.

"Are you okay?" he asked, sounding calmer than he had been.

"I'm fine. You?"

"When I shift, my emotions run closer to the surface, but I'm better now."

"Makes sense," I said. It didn't matter. Most important was he wasn't revved up to a ten anymore, and neither was I. We'd both seemed to reset in the last few hours.

He took a branch and poked at the fire. "Are you hungry? I can go get us something to eat."

"I'm okay. I ate some protein bars."

He then moved about the camp, and I tried not to haunt his every step with my stare. He finally settled down, making it easier to keep track of him.

He stared into the fire. "Is Blondie dead? I heard her body drop."

Wrong or right, I hadn't planned on telling anyone what had happened to Blondie, especially not him. It felt like adding another brick in the wall that was going up between us, partially by my doing. I wasn't in the mood for wall building tonight, or seeing the look of distrust that was going to come with it.

"She's dead. Not intentionally, but yes."

He nodded.

This wouldn't be the end. I waited, knowing it was coming.

"How did she die? Do you know?" he asked, proving me right.

"No," I said, hating the lie I couldn't stop myself from saying.

He turned my way, looking as distrustful as I feared. At some point I might feel bad enough to divulge my secret, but not yet, not when I still couldn't wrap my head around what I was becoming.

"You're lying. I know you're lying. Even if I didn't see it in your eyes, I can smell the lie on you. You know something about what's happening and you won't tell me."

He was staring at me so intensely that I almost caved and told him everything. I *wanted* to tell him until I imagined the shock, aversion, and disgust he'd feel. He'd run away from me as fast as he could because it was the only sane thing to do.

He could've trusted the old Piper, the one who would've told him what was going on. Not the thing I was becoming.

"I can feel the change in you," he said. "I'm not just talking about picking up on your moods. I can physically sense it."

He waited, as if he thought this would make me talk. It didn't. He thought he wanted to know what was wrong. He didn't. I knew, given the choice, I'd have no part of this.

"I didn't imagine our relationship would ever be like this," he said, sounding as if he were giving up on me.

The words felt like someone taking a sledgehammer to whatever hope I had left in me. I stayed silent because I couldn't bear to speak at this point.

He continued to stare at me, but I wouldn't look at him. It was too hard. I didn't know what to say, how to tell him what I was becoming. I didn't want to see the revulsion in his eyes. I'd rather he think I was too screwed up to trust him than know the truth. Somehow even that seemed better than telling him.

"I won't come back to the pack with you. I just need to figure out where I'm going," I said a few minutes later.

"You can't leave. You'll be dead," he said.

"I won't, and it's not your problem anyway." I'd make it work. One way or another, I'd have to.

"I don't walk away from my obligations."

Now I was an obligation? An *obligation*. I wasn't anyone's problem or burden.

"You don't have to. It's my choice," I said.

"I didn't—"

"You want to talk about secrets?" I said. "What about the bullets that bounced off you? What was that? I know shifters are tough, but that was definitely not normal. And why is it you're the only one who's not afraid to touch me? I'm starting to think you might be withholding as well." I locked eyes with him and didn't waver. I'd been so busy feeling guilty about not telling him everything that it had never occurred to me that I might not be the only one hiding things.

"I guess we'll both be keeping our secrets," he said.

"I guess so."

Chapter Twenty-Three

KICKS SLOWED THE BIKE.

I got off, looking around the dense forest and taking the opportunity to stretch my legs. "Are we close?"

I hadn't been in California since my mother died. With everything else happening, it didn't seem to hit me until now. Somehow New York falling hadn't hit me as hard as coming back here, with her gone and the place I'd lived most of my life destroyed.

"We're about an hour away, but I wanted to talk to you before we got there."

I was beginning to dread anytime someone wanted to talk to me. It was never good. Maybe being surprised by whatever bad thing was coming was better? The bad might still come, but at least I wouldn't dread it until it happened.

"What's wrong?"

"Several of our members have family over at the California pack, and vice versa. As you know, word gets out. After what happened, there is going to have been some chatter. I'm not sure what kind of reception we'll receive."

"*We*? You mean *me*. I'm pretty sure I'm the one they won't be happy to see."

"Whatever the case, don't wander off on your own, and I want you to be on guard."

"Got it." I grabbed my canteen off the back of the bike. "I'm going to fill up before we get moving again."

I moved toward the sound of the water, looking for a few minutes alone.

Kicks didn't follow right away but appeared a few moments later, finding me kneeling beside the river and staring off into the distance.

"Is there something else?"

"California holds a lot of memories for me."

So much had happened in the last month that it was strange when I realized how little we really knew about each other. I'd had decades of life before him. He'd had... I didn't even know how old he was. Life had been such a constant battle since Death Day that what had come before was beginning to feel like it didn't exist most days. Even when it did, it didn't matter. And then there'd be times like this, where you couldn't see beyond all the ghosts of your past.

"I thought you were from New York?" he asked.

"I was born in New York, but I lived most of my life in California."

"Did you have family there?"

"I did." There didn't seem to be a reason to tell him my mother had passed from cancer before Death Day stole so many other lives. That would only irritate a wound that still hadn't closed.

I still wasn't sure what was worse—someone passing so suddenly that you felt that you didn't get a chance for goodbyes, or watching them slowly slip away bit by bit and not being able to do a thing about it.

Kicks watched me but didn't press for anything else.

"I'll be at the bike," he said, giving me my space.

Once we got back on the road, it didn't take long to get there. We rolled up to a gated development in a high-end California suburb with a couple of guards at the gate.

"Hey, Kicks. How's it going over in Arkansas?" one of them asked, looking happy to see him.

"As good as anywhere else," Kicks said.

"Yeah, I hear you there," the guard said. "Okay, well, head on up. Nix is expecting you. Third house on the left."

The other guard didn't say anything, hanging back a bit and then opening the gate at the signal.

I didn't miss the way they stared at me as we drove up through the gates. They hadn't only heard some gossip— they believed it.

Nix looked a little older than I'd expected, but still in his forties if he were human. With his thick, wavy golden hair and perfect build, I had to wonder if being attractive was an alpha requirement. Or did it just go hand in hand with their strong genetics?

"Come in. I just put some coffee on," he said.

We went into Nix's house, which looked exactly like I'd expect from a high-end build around here.

He waved us over to a sitting area in the room, making a concerted effort not to stare. He was most definitely sizing me up, though, and weighing if I were a threat.

He poured us both some coffee, bringing over a plate of pastries as well.

"Where's your mate?" Kicks said.

"She went up north, hunting with her brother."

He'd known we were coming. Had he been trying to get her out of here before I arrived? Or was that just paranoia setting in? It was hard to know at this point.

"She wanted to be here to meet you, but it's a family tradition that they go this time every year," he added.

Definitely not paranoia. He'd sent her away. I would've too if I were him.

"I like the new place. You've got a good setup here," Kicks said.

"The narrow roads make it easier to protect, although we're going to have to eventually move again. Right now we're running on generators, but we'll be out of fuel eventually and have to set up something closer to what you have. Any word from those humans setting up that oil rig?"

I nearly spat out my coffee. The two men looked at me. "Wrong pipe," I managed to get out.

"I wouldn't count on that, at least with the same crew," Kicks said. "Might be a bit before that situation is ironed out now."

Nix nodded, obviously fluent in reading between the lines. "Well, there'll be another. Maybe one of the packs will have to take a crack at it—not that I wanted to."

"Maybe," Kicks said, sounding as if he weren't looking to get into that either.

There was an awkward stretch of silence as Nix seemed to be figuring out how to broach a topic. "You seem decent enough, and I hope you get whatever answers you need from our guide," he said. "But for the sake of the stability and well-being of my pack, I'd like to ask you to limit your stay to as short as possible. Groza has been planting seeds throughout, and it makes things difficult."

Kicks reached out and took my hand, making his stance

clear. Even if I wanted to pull it away from him, I couldn't. He had a death grip on me. He'd probably break my fingers before he'd let go.

"I understand. I appreciate your allowing us to come here at all."

Was that a "thank you" Kicks had just uttered? Because if I hadn't understood the words, the tone would've been more suited to a "go fuck yourself."

"Kicks, you're an alpha. You understand the need to protect your pack," Nix said.

"I do. We'll be out of here as soon as we can." Kicks stood, pulling me up with him. "Just point us in the right direction and we'll do what we need and get going."

Fifo, the California guide, was standing on his porch as we walked up. If alphas were genetically inclined to be attractive, guides seemed to be on the other end of the spectrum. It wasn't so much that he was ugly, just an odd-looking little man. His nose was easily twice the size of what would be considered normal, and his eyes specks in comparison. He nodded to us both and then ushered us into his home in an overly jovial way.

I wasn't sure if he'd been assigned to this house or if he'd chosen it, but everything about the place was a shock to the system when compared to Jaysa's dark cabin. The windows ran floor to ceiling, and although they had drapes on either side, they weren't drawn. Plants lined the walls, big, tropical-looking things that filled the air with a fresh, clean scent.

"This is quite beautiful," I said.

"Did you think I'd choose a black hole just for theatrics?" He laughed softly. "Jaysa was a hack. She needed all the bells and whistles to scare people into thinking she was mightier than she was." He turned to Kicks. "Would you mind giving us some time alone? Some conversations are easier one on one."

Kicks looked at me.

"Go ahead. I'll be fine." It wasn't a line. There was something about the energy around Fifo that put me immediately at ease.

"I'll be waiting nearby," Kicks said, then left.

Fifo walked to the couch and sat. "Please join me?"

The couch wasn't that big. Did he really want me to sit that close to him?

I took a tentative step, but then paused, as if to be certain.

"Come," he said, patting the seat.

I did, and there were only a couple of feet between us. "You're not afraid of me?"

"I'm a guide. I can sense a threat, and you are not one." He gave me a kindly smile.

He could? I couldn't. He'd called Jaysa a hack. Maybe I'd gotten bad magic?

"There aren't many of our kind, and never one such as you before," Fifo said. "I think it best if you tell me what happened slowly, walk me through everything, even your life before."

"Before I was turned into this?" I wasn't sure I should call myself a guide anymore, considering I wasn't sure what was happening to me.

"Yes. From what you remember of your childhood and also of your parents. No human has ever had a guide's gift transferred to them, so I think we should start as early as you can remember. We didn't know it was possible. Now tell me about your life. What's been happening?"

I ran through most of it, which, up until recently, wouldn't have shocked most. It hadn't been a perfect life, but nothing out of the ordinary.

He nodded, asking follow-up questions here and there. Some of them seemed more nosy than meaningful, but I went along with it until there wasn't much left to be dissected.

"So no missing members in the family tree you know of?" he asked.

"My father was mostly absent, but not missing," I said. "I really don't know much of his lineage, though, so hard to say if there was someone missing in the tree."

He nodded. "I have a theory on why ten percent of humankind lived. It can't be proven, at least not now with our limited abilities, so I hesitate to share it often, but I think, given your position, I should tell you. It might help to unravel this situation a bit if I'm correct. At this point, you realize that this world is full of creatures and races you might not have suspected existed."

"I didn't know for sure, but yes, I'm coming to realize that." After all, if there were shifters, there had to be others.

"Shifters had a loss, but only about half, where humans nearly got wiped out. I believe that the ten percent of humankind who survived had genetics from other races that allowed them to make it past what happened on Death Day. That anyone who did survive has some sort of other DNA in them."

"You're saying I have some sort of shifter bloodline in my family tree? I didn't think shifters could have children with humans."

"I believe you're correct, but it has happened," he said, excitement in his eyes, as if he'd been dying to share this information with me. "And it might not be just shifter blood. Every creature you've read or heard about has some basis in reality, and it's been very common for them to dabble with humans. Even if only one mating in a thousand produces offspring, with billions of people over thousands of years, that adds up. After all, many human genetic changes started with a single mutation in one person that was beneficial."

"Would that affect what I might be able to do as a guide?" Was that why I could see the dead? Was this magic interacting with something in me that got all jumbled up?

He stared at my hands that were clenched in my lap. It was a position I now found myself in more often than not. "May I touch you? I'd like to see if I can get a read off your energy."

"I'm not sure I'm comfortable—considering, you know…"

His hands hovered near mine. "I'm not concerned. This might help give you answers, and you won't kill me."

"Are you just saying that, or do you somehow know that?" I asked. I wasn't sure I'd believe him even if he said he was sure.

"I've seen myself in visions beyond this moment. You won't kill me."

Visions? He got visions and I got dead people? Talk about getting screwed.

"If you're sure." If this guy dropped in front of me, it would be pretty damning. How many times could someone die around me before the packs all put a hit out on me?

Still, I'd come here for his help. If he insisted this was the way, how could I decline whatever he asked? He knew the risks. Could see how terrified I was, and yet he still wanted me to do this.

I held out my hands. He didn't hesitate and grabbed both.

An immediate connection flowed through our grip, and I yanked my hands back, jumping from the seat. I waited for a sign of his imminent death, cursing that I'd allowed him to convince me this was a good idea.

He sat calmly, watching me.

"I'm unharmed," he said after a few moments had passed.

"What was the feeling? There was a surge between us."

"We're both guides of the pack. We are connected because of this. Our energy levels run stronger and beyond what is normal, so when we touch, there is a sharing of sorts. That is why I need to connect with you to get a sense of what is happening." He motioned to the spot beside him again. "Please, it's all right."

He still hadn't convulsed or turned gray. Maybe he *did* know what he was doing?

I sat beside him again and slowly reached out. I tried to act as calm as he seemed, but there was no way he couldn't see the trembling in my fingers.

"Be at peace. You will not harm me." He gently sandwiched my hands between his, and that same scary flow of energy commenced.

Calm. Stay calm. If I feared—

No, don't even let your thoughts go that way. Don't invite them into your brain where they could—

I was doing it again. Forget focusing on staying calm. I had to keep my brain empty.

I hadn't realized I'd squinted my eyes closed until I found myself curious about what was happening. Fifo's grip was still warm and strong.

I opened my eyes to slits, as if only seeing a tiny bit of him dying would lessen the terror. His eyes were completely closed, but his skin was still a healthy hue.

I opened my eyes fully, finding myself transfixed by his expression. His head was tilted back and his lips were parted, as if he were in some sort of meditative state.

After a few minutes, I wondered how long we would do this. After ten minutes, I began to wonder if this was normal. Did I speak to him? If I startled him, would it trigger something? A bad chain reaction? What if I got jolted and he did something to frighten me, and then I killed him?

After another ten minutes sitting there, I was fidgeting in my seat. Did I rip my hands away? What was he doing? What was he sensing?

"Fifo?" I whispered, then stared hard for a sign he'd heard me.

His eyes might've squeezed shut a bit tighter, but I wasn't sure. It wasn't enough of a movement to be a real reaction. Maybe his eyes were itchy?

"Fifo?" I spoke louder this time.

He took in a gasp of breath and his eyes shot open. It was jarring enough that I tugged my hands back, just to be on the safe side.

He looked physically normal, but he stared at me with a strange look.

"You speak to the dead," he said. It wasn't a question. He *knew*.

"Are you all right?" I asked, afraid to offer any more details until I was sure he could handle this. It was one thing to talk to the dead. It was another to talk to *Death*. If he couldn't handle one, he'd never be able to handle the other.

"I'm wonderful. Through you, I was able to speak to

some of my deceased family." He hugged me before I could stop him.

I couldn't stand it for more than a few seconds before my nerves got the best of me.

"I have a question, but I need to know this stays completely between us."

"I would never betray the trust of another guide. What did you need to tell me?"

"These deaths that keep occurring around me—"

"I don't know why Zetti passed, but it wasn't you," he said. "Nor the last two."

"How do you know?" I asked. *I* knew Death had done it, but how did he?

He leaned back, looking more serious. "Death leaves marks upon the people around them, and I can sense from that whether you had any part in their passing. They didn't leave a stain upon you."

"But what if something was channeling what I can do? Is there a way to block that?" I clasped my hands in my lap, trying to appear calm even as my mouth grew dry and my pulse hammered.

"What could channel your gifts?"

As soon as he asked the question, I knew he wasn't going to have any answers on how to rid myself of Death. This trip had been for nothing. I hadn't had much hope, but now it was completely gone.

"I don't know. It just seems odd the way they died," I said. If he couldn't help me, sharing what was happening only opened me up to more problems. It was one thing for him to repeat that I spoke to the dead. It was another if he ever divulged that Death was using me to kill people.

"Be at peace. You didn't kill those people."

"Thank you." I tried to smile, pretending he'd helped, even as I scrambled to figure out what would come next.

I was barely off the stoop when Kicks crossed the street toward me. He motioned toward a small house across the street, then walked into it without knocking.

"Whose house is this?"

"No idea." He shut the door behind us. "Did you get any answers?"

I ran through what Fifo had said, and Kicks didn't look any more relieved than I felt. Although Fifo might've had some interesting theories, in the end he'd been useless to me. Other than thinking I wasn't ultimately responsible for the deaths, he had nothing that was going to fix my situation.

Kicks let out a long sigh. "We'll figure something out," he said, as if to fill the silence.

He didn't look too optimistic, and I definitely wasn't. There was only one thing left to do. It was time to cut ties before the situation got worse. I wouldn't do it here, though, and I wasn't going to slink off in the middle of the night. He deserved a goodbye at the very least.

"If you don't mind, I'd rather not stay here tonight. These people don't want me here, and I don't want to be here."

Kicks immediately tensed. "Did someone say something to you?"

"Not at all. I just want out of here." After how Nix had acted, as if he were doing us a favor allowing me here, I didn't want anything from them. I'd rather be sleep deprived than stay here another minute.

Chapter Twenty-Four

CONSCIOUSNESS CAME SLOWLY WRAPPED in my cocoon of warmth, the sun streaming through the trees and the birds chirping. It was so nice I didn't want to fully wake, but to stay in this feeling forever. Reality wouldn't let me, as Kicks' scent breached my peace and caused a well of panic to burst through me.

I realized why I was so toasty and comfortable and quickly rolled away, getting to my feet. "What are you doing? Why were you snuggling with me?"

Kicks sat up, stretching. "You were curled up into a ball, shivering. What was I supposed to do?"

"You should've let me freeze. How many bodies do you need to see turn gray? People drop like flies around me. You can't do that!"

"Your teeth were rattling so loud it was keeping me awake." He got to his feet, cracking his neck, as if he didn't have a care in the world. "You won't kill me," he said on a yawn.

"And why are you so sure?"

"Because you like me." He smirked.

I wasn't sure if he remained untouched because *I* liked him so much or because *she* liked him. If it was her, that could change in a second. Death struck me as a fickle bitch.

"This isn't a joke. I could've killed you." I looked down, making myself busy looking for embers to smother in a fire that had been dead for hours.

"Pips, it's okay," he said, shedding the teasing tone. "You're not going to hurt me."

"Yeah, sure." It wasn't okay, and after yesterday, I wasn't sure anything was going to be okay.

For a little while there, I'd thought that even if Kicks and I didn't end up having a love story, we'd at least have a decent life together. Maybe a friendship and peaceful existence. It had been a foolish thought. Before him, I'd thought I was going to be able to make a life at Groza's pack. I was beginning to think of my life was a stand-up routine for God. He was probably laughing in the aisles at this point.

I tossed down my stick and turned to face Kicks. I'd barely spoken last night. It was pointless to even continue on with him today. I knew what had to happen. There was nothing left to do but get the hurt over with.

"I'm not going back with you."

He'd been rolling up the blanket but froze. "What are you talking about? Of course you are."

"No. I'm not."

He looked too surprised to be hurt yet, but that would come. Unless he felt relieved. Either way, by the time this conversation was done, he'd probably be grateful I'd left of my own devices.

"You'd leave Charlie?" He spoke to me like he didn't even know who I was.

"I have to." My voice cracked.

What else could I do? I couldn't stop her, or her plans. What would happen if this stole all my humanity and left nothing but a monster? What would become of Charlie? My leaving might be the only thing that would save him.

Kicks took a few meaningful steps toward me. "I won't leave you out here alone, so you better tell me what's going on."

I'd had a feeling that this was the way it would go down. He really wouldn't let me go until he heard the horrible truth. It was the only way he'd see this was the way it had to be. In truth, I'd wanted to tell him for so long. The only thing restraining me was the fear of his knowing what haunted me. The disgust I'd see in his eyes.

"You're right. You have to know." Keeping it from him wasn't going to change it. No, it was time to deal with the inevitable. "I need some guarantees before I tell you." I sat on the nearest boulder, feeling defeated because that was what I was. By telling him, I was accepting the fact that I wasn't going to be able to stop her. I'd lost.

"I'll try to do whatever you need," he said, not hesitating.

I'd known he would. He'd probably do what I needed without my asking because that's who he was. Part of me needed to hear the words anyway. I didn't want an ounce of doubt in my mind that Charlie would be taken care of.

"I need to know you'll take care of Charlie, protect him like he's your own." Kicks would be a good dad. He'd do what he had to for Charlie, protect him. Hell, he'd probably thought I was killing off his pack, and he'd protected me.

He grabbed my shoulders in a firm grip, dragging me up. "What do you imagine is going to happen to you?"

"I need you to promise to care for Charlie first, and then I'll tell you everything." I had to have those words from his lips. He'd honor his promise, no matter what he might think after he heard the truth. He was honorable, much more than I'd ever realized or could've hoped for.

"I give you my word I'll care for him. Now tell me why you think you won't be around." Kicks was still holding me, and it was clear he wasn't letting go until I spilled everything. "Pips, *tell me*."

"I didn't kill Zetti or Louise, and it's not a guess or because Fifo said it. I *know* I didn't."

Here was the tough part. How much could one person hear before they went running and screaming from you? I didn't know when it had happened, how it had happened, but he'd become my anchor, my security, my comfort. I didn't want to see him look at me with revulsion.

"You might not believe this, but I've wanted to tell you since the moment I knew. I'm not sure you'll want to hear it, though." I wrapped my arms around myself. "It's...terrifying, and that's coming from someone who lived through Death Day and can kill with a touch. I'm not exaggerating this." He'd want to know, just as I would. Kicks wasn't one to stick his head in the sand. It was one of the things I admired and respected about him. He'd take the hard truth, no matter how ugly, over a prettily wrapped-up lie. It was more of a warning to prepare him for what I was sure he'd choose.

"Tell me anyway," he said.

I looked around, wondering if Death would appear, and decided it didn't matter anyway.

"Shortly after the ritual that changed me, the one we did in Groza's garden, something happened. In addition to seeing some dead people and being able to kill people, I started seeing something that wasn't a ghost, that wasn't ever human or shifter or of this world."

I shuddered, thinking back to the first time I'd seen Death, walking toward the dead body. It seemed even worse now, maybe because part of her was inside of me.

"I'm not sure what you'd call her, but I call her Death. Maybe most would call her the Grim Reaper. I don't know what her true name is, as I've never asked. I hear her when she's coming, and then I see her go to the dead and collect their souls. But she doesn't just come for them anymore. She talks to me as well. She's the one who's been killing people around me."

He let go of me and stood still for a second. He didn't look scared, exactly, but he was a far cry from his typical at-ease appearance.

"You're saying *Death* killed my pack members?" he asked. "You're sure this thing you're seeing is Death?"

It sounded insane. Maybe he wouldn't think of me as a monster, more criminally insane. Was that better or worse?

"Yes. I'm sure." I hadn't thought I'd have to convince him. I'd been so concerned with his being disgusted or terrorized, his not believing it had never occurred to me.

"When do you see her?" he asked. He ran a hand over his shadowed jaw.

What if I couldn't convince him? Then what? How did I prove this?

"I've seen her every time someone has been about to die in my presence, except the ones she killed through me or I killed. When I hear those steps, I know someone is about to pass on." I shuddered just thinking of it.

"You know she's coming *before* someone dies?"

I nodded. "I hear booming steps before it happens. It's like hearing the footsteps of God, it's so loud."

He tilted his head slightly, narrowing his eyes. "Wait a second. That's how you knew my guy was going to die at that dinner when he had the accident?"

I nodded, having forgotten that he'd picked up on how spooked I was that night.

His lips parted on an almost-silent gasp. It was a small enough sign but the equivalent of someone else shrieking. I'd finally found something that shocked Kicks.

"So...Zetti?" he asked.

"Death wanted it to look like me, but she killed her. She killed Louise and Blondie too. She kills anyone she thinks might be a threat to me. She wants me alive so she can use me."

Kicks looked at me then took a few steps to walk about the area, trying to digest it all. He could have days if he needed, because this was one tough pill to swallow.

He finally turned back to me. "I just want to make sure I'm very clear on this. She didn't just collect Zetti's soul, but actually killed her?"

"She *killed* her. She wanted her dead, and she killed her."

"Do you know why she'd want to set it up to make it look like you were killing these people?" It seemed like he was going along with what I'd said, but he was definitely struggling down the path as he went.

"She wanted these deaths to look as if they were caused by me. She wants to use me as a tool to send a message. I guess it's a little hard to do that when you can't communicate directly." The more I told him, the easier it felt. I'd been holding on to this for so long that letting it go was like shoving an elephant off my chest.

"What message?" he asked.

Each new part he heard might be one more step toward his disbelieving me, and yet I couldn't stop talking now. I wanted it all out there.

"She said that the people behind Death Day took something from her. I don't really understand anything about that, but it's what she said. She wants to use me somehow to get retribution or revenge. I don't know every detail. It's not like I seek out these conversations with her. When I do see her, I want her to leave as soon as possible."

He nodded. "What exactly did she say? Repeat everything you remember."

I tried to go through every conversation I'd had with her, repeating it as best as I could. By the time I was done, Kicks was sitting on a fallen log, looking as confused and confounded as me for once. It was a lot better than the disgust I'd expected. It was almost nice to have someone experience the overwhelming nature of this situation with me instead of feeling like I was out there drifting alone.

Kicks was silent for a while, and I sat down on a log, waiting for him to come to terms with it all.

Then he was up again, taking a few steps around as if it would help him figure this out. "The other deaths, were they her as well? The ones back at Groza's?"

"No. Those were me." Lumping them in had occurred to me for a second, but did it matter at this point? The whole mess was a nightmare, no matter what column the check went in.

"It was only a question, and don't think for a second I'm judging you for them," he said softly. "If you want to know the truth, I'm glad you can kill like that. That you can defend yourself. It puts my mind at ease."

I watched him, trying to catch a glimpse of some hidden feelings. "I don't understand why you aren't revolted by me."

"Why would I be?" he asked, as if that question stumped him more than anything else I'd said.

The relief of getting it all off my chest was fading as the reality of leaving Charlie rushed in behind it. And leaving Kicks. *That* reality was hurting worse than I'd imagined. I grabbed my canteen, taking a sip and wishing it was whiskey or something stronger to numb some of the pain.

"At least you see why I have to leave now," I said.

"I'm not letting you leave. It's a death—"

"Sentence?" I scoffed. "No one is killing me. She'll keep me alive." I wouldn't be dead until she was done with me. I wasn't sure what would be left of me at that point.

"No. We'll figure something out," he said, as dug in as ever.

I'd never met anyone more stubborn than me until him.

"There is no figuring this out. What happens when there's another death? And another after that? I'll be driven out or killed. Well, *attempted* to be killed." Who knew how many people Death would kill if she perceived them as a threat? She wanted me and was going to use me whether I was on board with her plans or not. That was the problem. There was no way out of this. I was trapped.

He froze. "You really think that I'd let anyone threaten you?"

"What are you going to do? You're their alpha, but a pack has its limits. Someone else will die. There's no stopping her. She's going to do this, and she's going to use me." I got to my feet, standing in front of him.

"You're my mate. If you leave, I leave. There's no negotiation." His hands were on my shoulders, as if he thought I'd try to run now.

"Why do this to yourself and your pack? You need to let me leave." It was hard enough to do it when I didn't want to. Fighting for him to let me leave was sapping my strength to do it.

"I can't. Don't ask me why, but I can't." His whole body was tense, and I didn't doubt that he'd fight me if I tried to leave.

Maybe it was his honor. Maybe he did care for me to some degree. No matter what the cause, it didn't change anything.

"You know this isn't going to work."

"There's someone in New Mexico we need to go see. It's a long shot, but I think we should go there before any decisions are made."

"Who is it?"

"Someone that might be able to help. Like I said, it's a long shot, but we need to try it."

Was he grasping? The longer this dragged on, the harder it was going to be to leave. I barely had the strength to do it now.

"I just—"

His hands shifted into my hair as his mouth came down on mine. I'd never been kissed with such a raw intensity that it stole my thoughts, my will to push him away.

"We wait," he said.

"Okay." I nodded, knowing he was using everything in his arsenal against me, but I was too weak to walk away. I didn't *want* to walk away.

Chapter Twenty-Five

WE RAMBLED down a long dirt road, slowing the bike down as we approached our destination. The last rays of the sun gave just enough light over the landscape to make out an old warehouse looming about fifty feet away, surrounded by a couple of sheds and smaller buildings scattered around. The place didn't have much sense of life, and it looked like its better times had been long before Death Day.

I'd barely gotten off the bike when a man walked out of one of the smaller buildings. He was old, with a rounded belly and a long white beard. He could've been a mall Santa if he didn't have a rifle clutched in his hands.

"Kicks? That you?" he yelled from the distance.

"Dirkin," Kicks said. He walked forward, giving the old guy a hug.

"I can't believe you're here. I wasn't sure who was left, if anyone," Dirkin said, his voice steeped in emotion, which was at odds with his rugged appearance.

"It's so good to see you, Dirkin. I was afraid you were dead." Kicks gave Dirkin another pat on the back while reaching for me with his other hand. "This is Piper. She's my mate and also a guide." He wrapped an arm around my waist.

Dirkin's eyes narrowed, his nostrils flaring slightly. "She's…"

"Human," Kicks stated firmly.

Dirkin raised his hands in a placating gesture. "Not looking for a fight. Just surprised, is all. I didn't know humans could be guides."

"This one can," Kicks said, scanning the area. "Where is everyone?"

"Come on inside. I'll fill you in," Dirkin replied, motioning us toward the smaller building he'd come out of.

It was a small, one-room affair with a bed squeezed into one corner, a couch, and a small table with a couple of chairs taking up the rest of the space. Dirkin turned up an oil lamp that had been burning on low, casting a warm glow over the space. He waved us toward the sofa.

"I'll put some coffee on for us," he said, moving to a wood stove that looked like a recent addition to the place. "I've got some smoked jerky if you're hungry, too, but that's about it. The rest of us, the ones left, anyway, are out hunting."

"How many are left?" Kicks asked, settling onto the sofa.

Dirkin sighed, his shoulders sagging. "We lost about half the pack on Death Day, which was a helluva lot better than the human packs around here." He glanced at me and nodded. "Sorry about that."

"We all are," I said quietly.

"How's it been since?" Kicks asked.

"So, like I said, we lost half the pack. It was a tough hit.

Not to say it was easy on anyone, but we were never a big pack, only thirty or so," he explained, looking at me. "With so few of us left, it hasn't been easy. Groza sent an invite to come join her pack not long ago, and a couple of our people were grumbling about how it might be the right move. I'm not overly fond of her, but it might come to that." He shuddered and made a face like he'd stepped in horseshit. "I think I'd rather be left here alone."

"Groza isn't an option for us," Kicks said. "You could say that territory is scorched earth." He gave Dirkin the broad strokes of the situation, leaving out how many bodies I'd left behind.

"I'm sure glad to see you, though. Been wishing every day that I'd taken you up on that satellite phone offer," Dirkin said, handing us coffees.

"I'll get someone from the pack to run you one out after I get back," Kicks said. "I've been wanting to come check in on you, but there's another reason we came. I know you have connections with the *others* around here. I need to speak to one of them."

Others? What the hell did that mean? I'd had enough of any kind of *other*.

Dirkin whistled low. "You sure? We've got a lot of problems without looking for any."

"Yes. They might have information about some of the issues we're having."

"If you're sure, I'll give you a map. It'll lead you to their territory. As soon as you set foot beyond their boundary, there'll be no problem getting one to talk to you. Tell them I sent you. It will hopefully buy you a little grace, but not much."

What else was said seemed to fade from my numbing

215

mind as the mention of *others* lingered. Did I really need more problems? More unworldly creatures to contend with?

Dirkin pulled out some jerky. I didn't do much talking, still feeling numb, and I wasn't sure when that was going to wear off.

After a little more catching up, Dirkin showed us to one of the other small buildings. It had another retrofitted wood stove, which Kicks started loading up with wood, and a small cot in the corner we wouldn't be sharing. I couldn't even get nervous about that when I had too many other things to worry about.

"What are we supposed to be meeting, exactly?" I asked.

"It's sort of like a vampire—"

"What? You want me to meet a *vampire*?"

"Not the way you're thinking. They aren't pleasant, but they aren't what the movies would have you think. They don't go around feeding on people's blood until they die. They leech energy from humans, a little here and there, and people don't even know it's happening. A brush too close is all they need. They're integrated into the populace, living among humans, only taking the energy they need. You ever feel like you were dragging after a great sleep? It might've been them. I've never been a fan, but they don't bother shifters and we leave them be." He shrugged. "If there's someone who might have an answer, they're a good place to start, considering *she's* using your energy, in a sense."

I didn't want to meet these creatures. Like Dirkin said, didn't I have enough issues? But Kicks had a point. It was worth at least investigating when there were no other options on the table.

I sat down on the small cot, wondering how I was possibly going to sleep tonight, while he got the fire roaring.

Then he walked over, pulling off his shirt.

"We're not sleeping in this cot together," I said.

"Why not? Death isn't killing me. You said she likes me." He smirked, his eyes burning with heat. His stare alone was enough to send a surge of want through me. Sometimes when he looked at me, I felt like I was the only woman in the world.

"You think it's good that Death likes you?" I tried to keep my voice from betraying the heat building up inside of me.

"It's better than her disliking me, right? I think it's safe." He stood beside the cot, brushing my hair back from my face.

"She didn't say she liked you. She said she liked what you did," I said, leaning away from his touch.

"I'll take it." His voice was rough as he knelt on the cot. He shifted me backward until he was lying half on top of me.

I loved the weight of him on top of me, the smell of his skin and the feel of it under my palms, so warm and smooth.

"You know, it was easier to not do this when I thought you weren't ready. Now that I know it's because you think you're going to kill me, it's much harder to keep my hands off you." He smiled again, as if that had been good news.

"What if she changes her mind and kills you?" I whispered. It would be so easy to lose myself in him for the moment, but not when *she* wanted it.

"She won't." Even his voice, so low and gruff, seemed to heighten my arousal. He dipped his head, brushing his lips against my ear. "I'm *very* likable."

His hand ran up from my waist to cover my breast as his leg nudged mine apart and his thigh pressed against my core.

I arched into him, knowing that it would take almost nothing for me to absolutely fall apart in his arms. I'd never had this kind of connection to anyone, ever. The simplest touch from him and I was on the verge of losing myself.

Then that dark piece of me inside began to pulse to life, responding to his touch as well. I pulled away abruptly, scrambling off the cot and nearly falling in my urgency.

"I can't. I just can't." My voice broke, and I wrapped my arms around myself, trying to hold on to my resolve. "You don't understand. When you touch me, I can feel that piece of her coming to life. What if I lose control? What if what's in me hurts you?"

He stayed on the cot, concern smothering the fire that had been in his eyes a second ago.

"It's all right, Pips." He reached out, grabbing my hand and tugging me back toward the cot. "Just lie here with me. We don't have to do anything."

I lay down on the cot, settling in against his chest. True to his word, he didn't do anything else.

Chapter Twenty-Six

IT WASN'T QUITE noon as we stepped into the field that was technically *their* territory. Dirkin had drawn out the map this morning in between rolling his eyes and grunting.

"Don't let anybody who shows up get too close to you. They don't normally kill people, but that doesn't mean they won't or can't under the right circumstances," Kicks said.

Considering meeting this *creature* had been his idea, he wasn't selling it well. If I wasn't so desperate, I would've called the whole thing off. Unfortunately, I was near reeking of desperation. Sweat and dread was my newest scent lately.

"You don't need to warn me. I don't touch anyone intentionally, remember?" I couldn't imagine how anyone could forget.

He kept his eyes on the horizon but smiled.

"I'm glad you find my killing abilities a source of joy," I said.

"There's always a silver lining." He nodded to the other side of the field. "We've got company."

A man was walking toward us, tall and gangly, with whitish-blond hair.

As he walked closer, I could feel the difference in the creature who approached. I could smell a sweet scent from him, see the way his eyes twitched unnaturally. A year ago, I might've noticed him and thought him slightly odd, but wouldn't have given it much more thought than that. Now, I watched with eyes that felt like they were centuries older than the girl I'd been. Maybe it wasn't life that was making me more attuned but the piece of Death that had taken up residence in me.

As the man grew closer, his eyes seemed more intent on me, and he gave Kicks only a passing glance. He stopped a good distance away, scanning me.

"We're friends of Dirkin," Kicks said. "We don't mean to cause trouble. We've just come to talk."

"Who is she?" the man said.

I sensed he was more interested in *what* I was more than *who* I was.

"She's my mate, Piper. I'm Kicks. We're from the Arkansas pack."

"But *what* is she?" The stranger's gaze remained fixated on me.

"I'm a human that had guide magic passed on to me," he replied.

He hesitated but then nodded. That description was probably enough to confuse him and throw him off the scent of what else was going on. At least, I hoped. I still wasn't sure how we were going to ask for help when we didn't want to tell them what the problem was.

"What do you want?" he said, still not offering a name.

"We're having issues with certain outside energies

affecting her," Kicks replied. "Your race lives off energy, so we thought you or one of your people might be able to help us."

"Why would we ever help you after Death Day and what your people have done?"

Nausea welled in my belly, threatening to make me sick. Here was yet another source saying it was at least some of the shifters behind Death Day. Death had never specified exactly who was going to be traumatized and who had stolen some of her powers, but the fingers kept pointing to shifters.

"I lost half of my pack. I had nothing to do with Death Day," Kicks said like a man who was standing on a hill, ready to die.

"Maybe not you, but your people did. My kind needs humans, and your people did this, which jeopardizes our existence. You don't need humans the way we do. Instead of taking here and there from many, we're forced to drain them completely, making the situation even worse as we further deplete our life source. We're starving to death trying to keep from killing more. Another Death Day and there won't be enough left to sustain us, which might be what you all desired."

"We too have heard the stories. We're on the same side," I said, drawing the creature's attention back to me. "I'm still human. I lost many people that day. I would not associate with anyone that had a hand in Death Day."

He continued to stare at me while Kicks visibly bristled beside me. As off as this creature seemed in terms of human- ity, he didn't feel threatening. There was a sense that, deep down, he was as lost and desperate as me.

"Can you help? Please?" I asked.

He stood silently for another few seconds. I might've been imagining it, but his stare seemed to be softening.

"You will owe me a debt," he said.

Apparently not softening enough to not take advantage of the situation.

"Fine," Kicks said.

"*She* will," the man said.

"Fine," I replied.

Kicks was about to protest—I could see it on his face.

"I'm fine with it," I told him.

His jaw grew squarer, but he didn't say anything.

"The one you seek is close to here." The man pointed in the distance to a break in the trees. "Follow that path until you come to a small cottage. Tell her Hakas sent you. That will get her to talk to you, but you'll have to negotiate for anything else."

I was in debt for an introduction? If it worked, it wouldn't be so bad, hopefully. If it didn't, I was going to be really pissed off.

Hakas was gone before we even took a step, and I hadn't seen him leave.

The place wasn't far. Nestled deep in the woods was a small house that looked as if it hadn't had modern amenities even before the end of the world. A pack of dogs came rushing over as we approached. Kicks stepped in front and they suddenly stopped barking, with several of them rolling on their bellies.

"What did you do?" I asked.

"Told them I was boss," he said.

"Nice trick."

"I'm occasionally useful."

A woman walked out onto the small stoop, white-blonde

hair flowing about her. She had a face that was timeless and smooth, even as I sensed age. I wouldn't have been able to put an age on her if I tried.

"Hakas sent us. He said you might be able to help," Kicks said.

"Help you how?"

"I'm being haunted," I said, going with the closest thing to the truth.

It fit the bill if I downgraded Death to your random old spirit, meaning she just sort of hung around and wasn't using me to kill people. Yeah, "haunted" would have to work.

"I don't know if I can help you, but I can try," the woman finally said. "Come in."

The entire way to the place, I'd expected Death to appear, threatening me or doing something to stop me. At the very least, hovering menacingly. None of that had happened. As we walked closer to this woman, I expected something to stop me, but nothing did.

"I need to test you," she said as we walked in. Her small place was filled with counters and shelves lined with jars. Drying plants hung from the ceiling.

"Okay," I said.

"Test her how?" Kicks asked at the same time.

"I can sense something unusual about her energy, but I don't know what it is or where it stems from. I need to know the origin in order to fix it." She pointed to the center of the room. "Stand here."

She walked over to a bench loaded down with all sorts of jars and vines and began muddling several different items. She reached above to the ceiling, cutting away a clump of a dried plant, and then took the ingredients she'd been muddling and poured them over it. She turned back to me with a lit candle and her bunch of dried herbs, which she also lit. They flamed a strange red color before dying, smoldering with an almost silvery smoke that didn't smell like smoke at all but like a field of flowers. She circled me, waving the smoke in my direction. Every time she tried to wave it closer, it seemed to be repelled .

She made a little noise somewhere between a grunt and a hum as she moved her smoking wad of whatever closer to me. It still didn't seem to want to touch me, though.

"This is unusual."

I remained silent, afraid to glance at Kicks, fearing one look might give away everything. If she had the entire situation laid out for her, she might run me out of her house.

"You say you're being haunted. What exactly are you being bothered with? Is it spirits from your past?"

For the first time, it occurred to me this might not just block Death, but Widow Herbert and Jaysa. Losing Jaysa wasn't worth fretting about, but I wished I'd had a chance to say goodbye to Widow Herbert. Although if I didn't purge myself of Death's presence, I'd never see her again anyway.

"Yes. People from my past who haven't moved on."

She made another humming/grunting sound. "I'll mark you with a blocking protection spell. That should do it if that's all that is amiss." She stared at me, waiting for me to give some acknowledgement.

I nodded. That was as good as it was going to get, because if I opened my mouth, she'd hear the lie.

"It'll cost."

"What do you want?" I asked.

"Five years."

"Five years of what?"

"His life," she said, looking at Kicks.

224

"No."

"Done," he said at the same time.

"*No*." I stared at Kicks.

"Five years is nothing to me. It's worth it," he said.

"Fine." I turned my gaze back to her. "But with a guarantee of success?"

"Deal," she said. "I have to ink your skin. This won't hurt much other than the feeling of prickling." She lifted her hands and held them hovering over my body until she stopped behind me. "Here. It has to go here," she said, tapping the middle of my back.

"Do it."

She went back to one of the benches lining the room, gathering together her items. I could only imagine a prison tattoo setup would put her bowl and needle to shame. It didn't matter, as I wasn't looking for a piece of art but an act of magic.

"Take your shirt off," she said.

I pulled it off, glad that the few bras I'd been alternating were the pretty ones Evangeline gave me. It was sort of a ridiculous thing to care about.

As Kicks leaned a shoulder against the wall, staring at me like he wanted to ravage me, it didn't feel so stupid.

Our eyes met, and I could feel my body coming alive, barely paying attention to what the woman was doing—until she started making more humming noises.

The prickling feeling on my skin stopped for a moment. The pause didn't last long before it began again, only stopping a few seconds later.

"Is something wrong?" I tried to catch a glimpse of her over my shoulder.

"It won't take," she said, as if it were my fault. "What aren't you telling me?" She put down her needle tool.

"Try again," Kicks said, crossing the room toward us. "I'll pay you double."

I gasped. "No. That's too much," I said.

It didn't matter, as she wasn't having any of it. She was on her feet, pointing at the door. "You lied to me. Get out."

"Try again." Kicks wouldn't budge.

"Can you please try again?" I asked, my hunch telling me pleading was going to go farther with this woman, at least if her glare in Kicks' direction meant anything.

She turned that glare on me. "There is only one thing that would stop me from applying the block, and that is a connection to Death herself."

"Is there something I can do? Have you seen this before?" She knew Death was female, as if she'd also seen her or talked to her. I was ready to get on my knees and beg her for information if that was what it took.

"If Death singles you out, there is nothing that can break that connection," she said. "That is all I know. That is all I was taught. Now please. *Go*. I do not want that kind of attention in my life." She pointed toward the door again, looking as if she'd try to manhandle us out if needed.

Giving her the slightest nod, I took a step toward the door. I wouldn't damn anyone else to my hell.

I stopped beside Kicks. "She tried. We have to go. She can't fix this."

I should've been more disappointed, but there was one upside. His life wouldn't be cut short for me.

He hesitated for only a second before looking at me. "Okay."

We walked out of the place as a gust of air kicked up,

226

carrying an unusual chill. Death was here. The darkness inside me pulsed at her nearness. The dogs who'd been lying on the ground around the house whimpered and ran off.

Kicks looked at me as if he sensed something amiss as well but couldn't pinpoint the cause.

I shook my head, silently asking him to not press the subject.

Death appeared right beside me. "Did you really think that would work? I'd have killed her before she could do anything, even if she were capable."

I couldn't speak. I didn't want to alert him to her presence, unsure of how that would go, so I stared at her silently.

"You think what is happening is wrong," she said. "You're scared of what you might become, but I know this is the way. You'll be happy once it's done."

The way to what? Damnation? To become something so unholy I feared to be near others? I hadn't lied to Kicks. I'd fight, but it looked like a losing battle. If I was a betting woman, I'd put my money on her.

He stopped the bike a little bit later, after we were a safe distance away. I got off, knowing neither of us had a plan for what we'd do next.

Grabbing my canteen, I headed toward the river. Thirst didn't drive me so much as a craving for a moment alone to get a hold of my thoughts.

"I can see you losing hope. You can't give up," Kicks said, following me.

I could hear the agitation in his voice. I got it. He wanted to fix me. He still thought there was a way. There wasn't. How could he fight the forces at work when he couldn't even see them? No one could, only me, and I was at a loss.

He didn't understand. Letting me walk away was the optimistic end point. Killing me might be a safer bet, but he wouldn't do it. Even if he was willing, she wouldn't let him. She needed me and was going to use me whether I was willing or not, and damn anyone who got in her way.

"She's changing me. It started with Zetti. It wasn't much of anything, just this hint of emptiness in my chest. I thought it was all in my head. Then it grew a little more with the next death. It does something to me in a way I can't explain. It feels like it's eating away at who I am." I wrapped my arms around myself, feeling the shift inside me that I couldn't stop. "I don't understand it, but I can feel this different energy growing in me every time she does it. I'm afraid it's only a matter of time before I'm no longer me."

"You need to resist her," he said, walking closer until he was in front of me.

"Even if I don't give in, I can't stop her."

"We keep trying," he said, grabbing my arms.

I nodded, giving him what he wanted. I could agree with him every hour of the day, and it wouldn't matter.

"I'm not letting you give up. Buddie and Rastin are supposed to stay in Florida for a couple weeks. We still have some time to figure this out."

He walked away, staring off into the distance. It was what he did when he couldn't figure out an answer he was searching for. He wasn't going to find one. I knew where this ended, and it wasn't anywhere good. Death would kill anyone that could fix me.

"I need to talk to Charlie." If there was no way out for me, I'd at least make sure he landed somewhere safe. If I couldn't get Kicks to leave me, maybe that would be at Maddocks' pack with Buddie and Rastin for now. He couldn't come with me. Not like this.

Kicks nodded, locking eyes with me. "We'll figure this out."

I nodded again. I didn't have the energy to fight him. I had to save what I had left to figure out a plan for Charlie.

Kicks dug out the satellite phone, turning it on. He left it off most of the time, only turning it on to check in with the pack once a day, trying to conserve the battery.

"Hey, we wanted to check in on Charlie." He looked at me as they spoke. "Okay." He hung up and then handed the phone to me. "They're calling right back as soon as they get him."

The phone rang. "Charlie?"

"Hi, Piper!" Charlie's voice was like a beacon of light compared to my current mood.

"Are you having fun?" I asked, trying to match his enthusiasm, despite the disappointment I'd just been dealt.

"Yes! I went on two different roller coasters, and another ride that went over this city at night. They said they'd turn on the boat ride today."

"I'm so glad. Are you being good and listening to Buddie and Rastin?" I clung to the phone, as if it were a piece of him right beside me.

"Yes, I promise! Are you going to come here soon? It's so much fun."

I took in a deep breath, trying to make sure I had control of my voice before I answered. Kicks squeezed my shoulder.

"Piper?" Charlie said.

"Yeah, I'm here. I'm sorry. There was a bee. You know

how they scare me," I said, trying to fake a laugh to sell my lie.

"Are you going to come?" he asked.

"I told you I can't come this time. Right now Kicks and I are taking care of some issues, but maybe in the future?"

"Okay," he said, his voice a little quieter.

"So you like it there? You're going to have to tell me all about it." Even if I had to leave him, it didn't mean I wouldn't be able to talk to him. Even if Kicks wasn't with me, I'd find a way to get a satellite phone. And eventually this mess would get straightened out, even if it wasn't until Death finished me. I refused to believe I'd never see him again. I just hoped I was still enough of myself to care.

"I love it. Oh! Buddie says the boat is on." He was almost yelling in my ear, and I loved every second of it.

"Okay, go. Don't leave them waiting. I'll talk to you soon," I said, as it felt like my heart was being put into a meat grinder.

Kicks turned to me after I hung up. "I told Dirkin we'd be back tonight. We take a few days or a week to figure it out and decide what's best."

"Okay." I already knew what was best. I'd just have to convince him.

Chapter Twenty-Seven

KICKS WAS on one of the larger buildings, nailing in a piece of roof. He'd been at it for hours, helping Dirkin do a few repairs around the place. I wasn't sure why the people who lived here couldn't do them, but it didn't feel like my place to intervene. Plus the distraction was keeping us from the fight that we'd had every day for the last three days we were here.

We were supposed to leave tomorrow morning. Kicks still insisted we should go back to the pack, while I was steadfast that I was leaving him somewhere along the way. Maybe the place we'd stopped on our way to California? A place he knew. It would be a compromise of sorts.

I was so wrapped up in my thoughts that the thumping noise jarred me. I glanced over to where Kicks was working with Dirkin, expecting to see a piece of debris they'd tossed off the roof. Instead, Kicks was slumped on the ground.

I ran over, finding arrows littered all over his body. How had they even pierced his skin? I'd seen bullets bounce off him. Was it what they were made of?

"What happened?" I yelled, not even sure where Dirkin was as I knelt beside Kicks, who was barely conscious. "Dirkin!" I screamed.

Kicks mumbled something, but I couldn't understand him.

I leaned closer. "What?"

His eyes opened a little wider. "Run."

For a split second I did nothing, shock stealing my movements. Finally I got to my feet, grabbing his arms so I could drag him away with me, no plan other than getting out of the open.

I hadn't made it a foot before a loop of rope fell over my head and was immediately tightened. I'd just grabbed on to that when it was followed by another, both leaving only the slightest slack for me to get air. There were rods attached to the ropes, the kind of things they'd use on wild animals.

My hands were at the ropes tightening around my neck, forcing me to my feet and pulling me away from Kicks.

I tried to look around, spotting Dirkin standing off to the side and two men I'd never seen before holding the rods. Groza was approaching in the distance.

"What did you do?" I yelled at Dirkin.

"What needs to be done to protect my people," he said. "They told me about you."

I couldn't fault him for wanting me dead. But Kicks?

"He was your friend. How could you do this to him?" I pointed to Kicks' body on the ground, so lifeless.

"He made his choice," Dirkin said. "If you want to blame anyone, blame yourself."

I already was. I should've left days ago, left the pack as soon as Zetti died, but in my heart, I hadn't wanted to. Now Kicks was going to die because of me.

Groza appeared near me, Duncan beside her, along with some of the goons I remembered from her pack.

"No one believed I'd be able to catch you, but look at you now."

"You better let me go." Death was going to appear any minute, and she'd kill them. I wasn't sure if it would be enough to save Kicks, though.

"Or what?" Groza said, laughing. "The only ally you have left is dead."

I couldn't get close enough to touch them, but that didn't matter. Death would come. She'd kill my enemies.

Yet here I was, caught, and she wasn't anywhere to be seen.

"Death," I said, hoping it would prompt her arrival. She needed to get here before Kicks bled out.

"Yeah, I'm not so sure that's going to work, considering you can't move right now and your dog is lying on the ground."

"Death!" I nearly screamed. They thought I was threatening them. I was, but not in the way they thought. Where the hell was she?

"How many times do you plan on yelling that?" Groza asked, laughing again. "No one is dying but you two. The packs are all against you. Nix is the one who told us you were going to California. He sent someone out and told old Dirkin here to keep you put any way he could."

Had Kicks told Nix where we were heading? Had someone in that pack heard our plans? If that were true, why hadn't Nix done this when he had us there? No. It had to have been spies in his pack—not that it mattered. We were caught, and I wasn't expecting Nix to swoop in and save us, not after the slightly chilly reception we'd received.

I turned my attention to Duncan, hoping some of the man I thought I'd known was still in there. "Duncan, please, don't do this."

"I know you've killed again. I'm sorry, but you need to be put down." His face was like stone as he stared at me.

Had I ever really known him? I didn't recognize this person at all. Even his choice of words, like I was a rabid dog.

"Fine, you hate me. I'm a threat. I get it. But how do you do this to Kicks? He's done nothing. He's one of you. He's a shifter."

"A shifter who made bad choices," Duncan said. "He declared his loyalties, and they weren't with us."

"Then kill me. Then there's no conflict and you can let him go," I said. I was as good as dead anyway. But if I could save Kicks somehow...

"It's too late. He won't be manageable once you're dead," Groza said. She signaled to her goons. "Throw him in the hole."

I barely kept myself from heaving. The hole had been freshly dug by Kicks and Dirkin on the pretense of being a new well. Dirkin had made Kicks dig his own grave. I turned, meeting the old man's eyes. He'd be the first I'd kill.

They grabbed Kicks' arm, spinning his body and dragging him over the compacted dirt, leaving a trail of his blood behind. He didn't move, didn't even moan. I stared at him, watching for the rising of his chest. Searching for a sign of life. They got him to the edge of the ditch and then kicked him in.

A scream pierced the air, but it was mine. Kicks' only sound had been a thump when he hit the bottom.

Groza turned to me. "First I'm going to let you watch

your mate die. And then, once he's dead, I'm going to burn you alive in the ditch."

Why not kill me now? Why bother with this? Was there a reason, or did she simply relish the torture? Either could be true, and I wouldn't put the question to her.

"Throw her in. Try not to break her neck as you do, but if it happens, that's all right too," she said.

"No! She has to be burned," Dirkin yelled. "It's the only way to get rid of the demons."

They steered me closer to the hole. I would've jumped in to get Kicks. That was when I realized...I loved Kicks. There was no doubt in my mind. It was as clear as a switch being flipped.

They pushed me closer, and I held on to one of the poles attached to my neck, hoping to make it to the bottom in one piece. I fell in, and the nooses tightened for a moment, stealing all my air. Then they were released, pulled off and upward.

The well had been dug so deep it was darker down here. I knelt by Kicks' body, tears streaming down my face. I felt his head, trying to see if he'd taken a hit there. I didn't feel anything, but maybe it was too soon?

I grabbed his wrist, feeling for his pulse. It was there but thready. The first time I learned of shifters was when Buddie had been shot. He hadn't healed until he shifted. Was this the same? Did Kicks need to shift?

I needed him to wake, to ask how to help him. I needed him to live. He wasn't allowed to die. He didn't even know I loved him. All I'd done was push him away, and now he was dying and I wasn't sure if there was anything I could do.

I put my arm under his head, cradling him, kissing his cheek and then his forehead.

"Kicks, please, please don't leave me. Please." When he didn't answer, I looked upward. "Death! Please, I know you can hear me. Please, I'll do anything. I'll do whatever you want."

I waited, hoping she'd finally show, but nothing happened. I called her again, and then again. I cradled Kicks' body as close as I could, trying to give him warmth from my own.

"Death, please, *please* come."

Nothing. No answer as I lay there, feeling his blood seeping onto me.

"Kicks?" I laid my hand on his cheek. "Kicks? I need you to talk to me. You have to hang on. I'm going to get us out of here."

His breathing quickened slightly, and I felt him stirring.

"I'm here," he said, his voice weak and soft.

I shifted, moving to get into action. He was back with me. We'd figure this out. "What do I do? Should I pull the arrows out?"

"Yes. Out."

I knelt by his side, feeling around for each protrusion in the dark as best I could. As soon as I laid hands on the first one, I tried to feel for the angle it went in, and then tried to pull it straight out. He grunted softly as more blood gushed out behind it.

"Should I keep going?" If I did, would he bleed out? He'd bleed out if I did nothing, too.

"Yes."

"Okay." My hands were trembling. I was terrified I would kill him. I hung on to the memory of how Buddie bounced back when I'd taken the bullet out of him. It would be just like that.

I felt around for the next arrow, knowing there were four of them. I again found the angle, trying to pull it out while doing the least damage I could. Another surge of blood followed, and I dipped my head, ready to vomit. I breathed deeply until I settled again.

"Good?" I asked as soon as I could speak.

"Keep going."

I did the next two without asking him, just trying to get it over with. As soon as I got the last one out, I waited for him to shift, the way Buddie had, so he could heal.

He didn't.

I cupped his cheek. "Kicks, they're out. You need to shift."

"I'm trying," he said, sounding no better than he had.

Trying? Did that mean he couldn't? I was afraid to ask. I didn't want to worry him, or make him think I doubted he could. He was weak, was all. It was going to take a little longer, but he'd do it. He'd be okay. He'd get us out of this ditch and he'd be okay.

But as the minutes kept adding up, he kept lying there. He still didn't shift, and he sure didn't seem like he was getting better.

"Kicks?" I said. My voice cracked.

"I'm trying. I'm going to just rest for a few and then I'll try again."

I waited, letting him rest, hating that he had to. Buddie had shifted the second I got the bullet out of him. This was wrong. I arranged myself, trying to use my body as a pillow between Kicks and the cold, hard ground.

I ran my hand through his dark hair, giving him whatever comfort I could.

"Piper, we need to talk," he said an hour later.

237

"No. Not now. You're too weak. You need to rest until you can shift. Then we'll talk after we get out of here."

"Piper, I'm not going to heal. I thought it was just the arrows, but I think they had poison on them."

His words slammed into my brain, making me acknowledge how he'd been looking weaker and weaker by the hour.

"I don't know why you're saying that, but it's not true," I replied. "You just have to eat and rest and you're going to get better." No. He was not dying. This was Kicks. He was too tough to die. He was a shifter and an alpha. He'd heal.

"You have to listen to me. I'm dying. They threw me in here to die, with you witnessing. She's using me to torture you first, and then they'll kill you. But you still have a chance."

"You do too. Don't talk like that. Don't give up. It wasn't poison. It was just too much at once, and you'll come around."

"Listen to me. I don't have the strength to fight with you, and this is important," he said, his voice too soft for my liking.

"What?" I said, afraid if I argued, he'd waste precious energy on it.

"They'll come down to get me after I die. When an alpha dies, there are certain parameters that must be fulfilled within a certain time period or you're courting catastrophe. Dirkin is too superstitious to let them burn my body with you."

But they *could* kill him? I stayed silent, not wanting to make this worse.

"They'll have someone come and try to collect my body from above," he said. "You need to stop them from doing it so they have to come down with a ladder. It's your only hope. You need to be strong and take your chance escaping as soon as that happens. Even if I'm still breathing, you need to do it, because I'm as good as dead."

"Death is going to come," I said. I didn't know why she wasn't here yet, but she'd come. She wouldn't let me die, and hopefully it would be in time to save him.

"But she hasn't," he said.

"She will."

He flailed a hand, trying to reach for mine. I grabbed it and held it firmly to my chest, hating how cold his normally warm skin was.

"If she does, don't bargain for me. I can't live knowing what it cost you. I'd rather die."

If somehow she showed before he was dead, I'd give her anything, so I didn't speak.

"Promise me," he said, as if he could read my thoughts.

I still didn't speak.

"Promise," he said louder.

"Fine. I promise," I said, only to avoid drawing attention to us, afraid they'd shoot him again.

He settled down a bit, and I wrapped my arms around his torso, willing my strength into him.

Chapter Twenty-Eight

IT HAD BEEN HOURS. How many, I didn't know, but the sky had completely darkened and the moon was right above us, shedding light on Kicks' still body.

He wasn't going to shift. He wasn't going to get better. He was dying, and there was nothing I could do to stop it.

There had been laughter up above as they listened to me beg, threaten, and demand that the dying man in my arms live. Then they'd grown bored of the show and moved on while I listened to his breathing, waiting for it to stop.

With his head cradled in my lap, my legs had gone numb hours ago. I didn't care as I ran my hands through his hair, over and over again, trying to bring him some comfort or peace, or strength to fight—but mostly because I wanted to touch him, be near him in any way I could, while I could.

I'd watched my mother die, then the death of most of the human race. I couldn't watch another person die, especially not him. Not Kicks, who was always so strong. It was like watching a mountain crumble in front of me.

You will not die, I thought, trying to force my will upon him.

If I could kill someone with touch, why couldn't I save someone? I willed all my energy, everything I had, into him, trying to force my power into his body. But nothing happened. He didn't stir and seemed to slump down farther. No matter what I hoped or prayed for, nothing seemed to make him come around. If he died, I'd find a way to kill every single one of them.

The only reason he was here was me. If I hadn't been so stupid and foolish, I would've left in the night. Kicks wouldn't be here. If I'd left after the very first death at the pack, he wouldn't be here. I was the reason he was going to die. He might not be able to deal with the cost of what I'd be willing to pay, but I couldn't live with his death on my hands.

I'd made a promise that I didn't think I could keep, and I didn't care what the ramifications were. He wasn't dying if there was anything I could do about it.

I brushed a hand over his cheek. "You can't die. Do you hear me? I love you, and you can't die on me. You can't." Uttering the words aloud seemed to unleash a fresh stream of tears from me.

His lips parted on a slight moan, as if some part of him had heard me, was trying to fight for me, but he didn't have the strength left in his battered body.

"Death? I know you're somewhere nearby. Come and help me and I'll give you whatever you want."

I waited for her to appear in front of me like a genie to do my bidding. But it had been an idiotic thought, because nothing happened, as it hadn't all the other times.

I called her again and again. I continued calling her as

Kicks grew weaker in my arms. If I could've ripped open a vein and fed him my blood to save him, I would've.

I continued to call Death, even as all hope seemed to disappear and the tears were flowing like rivers down my cheeks.

The sky began to lighten as I continued my vigil. Kicks hadn't stirred at all for hours, and I could sense that his time was almost up. I'd held him through the night, praying that at some point something would kick in, that some part of what I had would save him. It was a desperate notion, but I *was* desperate. I couldn't think past his dying enough to even try to save myself. It was like a brick wall was erected in my mind, where there was Kicks alive and then there was nothing. I couldn't make it past his death.

But then I'd think of Charlie and knew I'd have to keep going, no matter how painful it was. I had to keep going for him, even if I was losing the will to do it for myself. I had to make sure he was somewhere safe. I'd trusted Kicks to do that for me, but now...

I shifted again, curving my body around his, trying to keep him warm so he'd have more energy to fight.

"Still alive, but doesn't look like for much longer," someone yelled from above.

I looked up, catching sight of the face so that I could memorize it when I got out of here and knew who to make sure I killed first. That dark part of me, the piece of Death that had continued to grow, seemed to awaken and prick up its ears at my bloodlust. I didn't care. I wanted it to grow if it would help me save him.

The shifter looked down, meeting my glare with a sadistic smile. "I hope I'm the one who gets to burn you."

243

The dark part of me swelled, pulsing to life, and I tried to encourage it.

The shifter smiled and then disappeared. Then my view was suddenly blocked by Death standing over me.

"I've been calling and calling you. Why didn't you come?" My words were laced with hard accusations, proving just how desperate I was. No one would speak to something such as her like that if they were in their right mind. I wasn't. I'd slipped into panic and desperation last night, and there was no coming back from it. I'd seen too much death in too short a time, and to see Kicks like this now was breaking me inside. I wasn't sure I'd ever be the same. He was the rock, the mountain that shifted gravity around him. From the moment I'd met him, he'd oozed life and vitality, pumping it out around him. Death hadn't seemed possible. Not for him. He wasn't supposed to die. He was supposed to be the last man standing.

"No human commands me." It wasn't a set-down. I didn't think she cared enough.

"You're not taking him." He was dying. Was that why she was here? To collect his soul? Because it wasn't going to happen. I'd fight Death herself if that was what needed to be done. His soul was staying right here with me.

I leaned forward, sheltering him from her view and making it beyond obvious that she couldn't have him. He was *mine*.

She stared down at him and then back to me, seeming bored. "You think you could stop me?"

The idea had flickered in my mind for a second. That I wanted him to survive enough that I could save him from even Death herself. I hadn't been able to save my mother, and Charlie had been saved by a minor miracle that was none of my doing.

She continued to stare at him. "He's nearly dead."

My grip on him grew tighter, as if I could physically keep his soul here with me.

Suddenly it all clicked. She'd told me one day I'd beg her. I was ready.

"You knew this was going to happen," I said.

"Yes."

"Can you save him?"

Death walked over, staring down at him. "I *could*."

She smiled, and it stopped my heart. Kicks hadn't wanted this. But it didn't matter. I couldn't let him go. I couldn't live with his death.

"You want your vengeance? You want me to do your bidding? Fine. You save him and get us out of here and I'll do whatever you want. But you don't get to take him. He's *mine*. No one takes him. *Ever*."

"I can live with this bargain. Can you?"

"I just said as much. Do. It."

I didn't care what the cost was. He was slipping away from me. There was no price too high. Even if doing this meant he'd no longer want me, I didn't care. He'd be alive, even if it was with someone else. But in order for me to go on living, I needed to know he was breathing, laughing, loving.

"Just know, the cost for cheating me is steep," she said. "You make the deal and you live by it."

I wanted to rage at her and tell her to go fuck herself, but I couldn't. Not until I was sure Kicks was safe, and probably not then either.

"I said do it." I didn't recognize my voice as I ordered

Death to do my bidding. I wasn't sure what the bargain I'd struck truly entailed, and I didn't care. I was becoming someone I didn't recognize, but it no longer scared me. I was becoming someone who would survive, and make sure those she cared about continued on, and that would be enough. It was more than enough.

She didn't touch him or kneel beside him. All she did was take a few steps toward him, and I could feel his heart-beat strengthening in my hold. He gasped, and his breathing grew stronger.

"He'll live," she said.

"You promised to get us out of here."

"I don't need to be reminded of my part of the bargain."

A stairway made of nothing but black shadows appeared beside me. Kicks was much larger than me, but I'd get him out of here if I had to drag him the entire way. I didn't want Death laying even so much as a pinky upon him.

"We're getting out of here, so you hang on. You hear me? We're getting out," I said.

Kicks didn't respond. His eyelids weren't even flickering.

I grabbed an arm in each hand, laying his body against my back, and he felt nearly weightless in my arms. Death was somehow taking some of his weight as I climbed the stairs that would lead us out of this hell.

The guards they'd posted at the edge of the hole whispered as they saw my head breaking level with the top of the hole. Their voices quickly grew louder, calling for help.

I didn't know if they could see the staircase of shadows or if it looked as if I were climbing the air. It was hard to guess which would appear more frightening.

"What the hell is going…"

I could see Groza staring at us as I took my first step out of the hole. Duncan was right beside her, but they both stopped short twenty feet from us, staring in horror. Their mouths opened in silent gasps, and no one came a step closer.

I looked at Death, who was right beside me. *What are they seeing?*

She smiled. "They're seeing you, or what you're becoming. They're seeing my vengeance materialize in front of their eyes."

I should kill them now, but then I'd have to put Kicks down, and I refused to part with him. Nothing, not even my vengeance, was more important than getting him out of here.

"Do you want them dead?" Death asked. "I don't care either way. He's clueless, and she's merely an idiot on the periphery, but this will serve its purpose."

There was no question when it came to Groza. I wanted her dead, and now.

Duncan was more complicated. I'd thought there would never be anything Duncan could do to completely turn me against him, not after he'd saved Charlie. I'd been wrong. There was a long list of things at this point, and the most glaring was what he'd done to Kicks. No amount of pleading had even made him think twice about the atrocity he was committing. If I didn't take him out now, he'd come for us again.

"Yes, I do," I said.

That was all she needed to hear, and what little weight Kicks was on my shoulders was lifted as his limp form slowly rose above me.

Groza and Duncan stood, terrified, watching Kicks' body rise above us. I took a step toward them, and they both turned to run but couldn't seem to get past some invisible barrier hemming them in.

Others were hiding but listening.

I turned to Groza. "You took something that wasn't yours to touch. You played a part in Death Day," I said, my voice coming out completely different than normal as Death's words were channeled through me.

There were gasps from the other shifters, loud enough that I could hear them even from their hiding places.

Duncan looked at her. "Is that true?"

"No, of course not." She was shaking her head, but she reeked of the lie.

"Now you, and all involved, will pay," I said.

She let out a gasp, and then raised her hand, showing its gray color.

"You don't deserve a fast death," we said, Death again channeling me for her purpose. "You will rot slowly for all to see, for the message to spread, that you do not take what is not yours."

"Please, I'm sorry. I didn't know what I was doing." Groza dropped to her knees.

There would be no mercy for her. I could feel Death's presence inside, the darkness in me swelling.

I turned to Duncan.

"I didn't take anything," he said. "I swear it. I don't even know what you're talking about. Please, Piper, don't do this to me. I got you out of New York. I saved Charlie. Please, for all that we had between us…"

He dropped to his knees as well.

"You tried to kill Kicks, and when I begged for his life, it fell on deaf ears," I said, my voice sounding more like my own, the words all mine.

"I messed up. I'm sorry. I shouldn't have done it. Let me go and you'll never hear from me again." He had his hands clasped together as he continued to kneel in front of me.

My emotions didn't even flicker. They'd shot Kicks with arrows and then thrown him in a hole to die.

"Because of Charlie, I give you the choice of a fast or slow death. Those are your only options. You will pay with your life."

He dropped his chin and then glanced at Groza, who was cradling her hand to her chest, seemingly succumbing to pain.

"Cutting it off will only hurry the spread," we said, Death's words coming through me again.

He looked me in the eye, as if in shock that this was what we'd come to. If only he'd shown some remorse and shock before he'd committed the atrocity.

"Your choices led us here. Not mine," I said. I would've forgiven him so many things until his attempted murder of Kicks. I wouldn't let that threat linger. I knew better now. I knew him better, and somehow, with Death flowing in and out of me, I could sense the rot in his soul. He wouldn't honor any word he gave.

"Decide or I'll choose for you," I said.

"Fast."

A second later, he was gone. I hadn't touched him. Death had done the dirty work, but it had been my call.

I stared at his dead body, regrets upon regrets piling up over how much had gone wrong. I wished I'd never met him. But then again, no. Because he had saved Charlie, and I'd suffer much worse than remorse and guilt for Charlie's sake.

The rest of the pack was still watching me from their

safe vantage points, but I had no fear of them. Death wouldn't let anyone touch me. We were acting almost as one now, and I felt safer than I ever had since Death Day, maybe even before.

I'd gained security but put my soul in peril. Even now, I could feel her power flowing through my veins, reaching out and caressing that dark piece of me, urging it to grow, to waken and enjoy the fruits of our labors. I was walking a thin line of holding on to who I was.

Groza was bent on the ground, still cradling her hand.

"You think this is the end?" she yelled, her face contorted in pain. "It's not. You're a dead woman walking. You won't live to see the year through. I promise you." She was screaming so loudly that spittle flew from her mouth.

"You definitely won't. My guess is you'll be taking your own life and being welcomed into hell by the end of the week," I said calmly.

"You're a monster!" she yelled. "You'll get yours."

She wouldn't be alive long enough, or well enough, to inflict anything upon anyone. Certainly not me.

"Where is Dirkin?"

"You want him dead?" Death asked.

"*Yes.*"

The old shifter was dragged by some invisible entity across the ground until he was at my feet.

"Do it," Death said. "Just wave your hand toward him."

I had a moment of flickering doubt, and then remembered his cold stare as his friend died. I waved a hand at him, and he was dead a second later.

I turned, catching sight of more shifters ducking back into their hiding places. I scanned the area for the few faces I'd put to memory but didn't see them.

Maybe I should've looked harder, tried to flush them out, but there was nothing I wanted more at the moment than to get out of here and take Kicks to safety.

He was hovering eerily in the air.

"Walk," Death said. "His body will follow. Leave the rest to spread the word."

I saw more shifters scurrying about, making sure they were nowhere in my path as I walked out.

I passed Kicks' motorcycle where it was still parked and continued to walk. I couldn't drive one of those things on my own, let alone with an unconscious Kicks behind me.

I continued to walk, heading into the dense woods, in the direction of Arkansas. I was going to bring Kicks home.

I walked for hours, Death flickering in and out of existence as I did. I finally stopped beside a river, and Kicks slowly lowered toward me until he lay in the dirt on the bank of the river.

I knelt on the ground beside him, hating how still he still was. "When will he wake?"

"Soon," she said.

I ran my hand over his face, brushed my fingers through his hair.

"So now what?" I asked, wondering what the full payment to her would entail but not caring. Kicks would live.

"We wait for word to spread, fear to grow, and then we strike again."

So there would be a reprieve of a sort, but this would be a long, slow mental war against all who did her wrong, until they were living in abject fear. Considering what they'd done to our world, they deserved it. Anyone who'd had a part in this was getting off easy, in my opinion. But by the time this was done, I wasn't sure what would be left of me. I could live with that, as long as the people I loved saw tomorrow.

It was hours I sat cradling Kicks' body by the river. Death had agreed to save him, yet he hadn't moved. I kept replaying the events in my head, trying to see if I'd made an error. If she'd saved him, why wasn't he moving? Why hadn't he opened his eyes? The sun was sinking in the sky, and I was beginning to fear that nothing had been negotiated at all.

I called out, "Death," as loud as I dared, but she didn't come.

At least his pulse felt stronger and his breathing was steady. I ran my hand over his hair again, as I had been doing nonstop for hours, hoping he could sense me, know he wasn't alone.

It was fully dark when he finally shifted in my arms. His eyes fluttered open, his brow furrowing as he woke somewhere different. I could see him trying to piece together what had happened.

"I'm alive," he said, sounding surprised.

"You are."

He lifted himself up into a sitting position, looking around. "Where are we?"

"I'm not sure. About a four- or five-hour walk from Dirkin's?" Or what had been Dirkin's. When I was waiting for Kicks to wake up, I hadn't thought about how I was going to tell him what happened. I hadn't cared. I still didn't, because it was the only reason he was alive. I had zero regrets.

He narrowed his eyes, trying to piece it together, as if he'd just forgotten.

"You couldn't have carried me this far," he said. "What did you do?" He was standing up, his movements stiffer than I'd ever seen.

I didn't speak, just got up and wrapped my arms around his neck. He didn't hesitate to hug me back, but I could feel the rigidness of his frame.

"Pips, what did you do to save me?" he asked softly.

I tightened my arms around him. "I struck a deal." My voice wavered. I knew how'd he'd feel about it.

His body could've been carved from stone for how hard he went.

He pulled back, and I didn't hang on. "What did you give in order to save me?"

I met his gaze. "Whatever she wanted, and I don't regret it."

His face fall. "Pips, you shouldn't—"

"Don't tell me what I shouldn't have done," I said, trying to keep myself together, but the damn tears started and wouldn't stop. It was as if every tear I'd managed to hold back was pouring out of me now. He didn't know what it was like watching him die, knowing it was my fault. How dare he judge me? "I'd do it again and again, no matter what the cost. Until you're in that spot, you don't get to tell me what I should've done until you're the one sitting there watching someone die and you know you can save them."

He nodded, taking me into his arms and tucking my head under his chin. "It's okay. Whatever it is, we'll figure it out. I won't leave you. We'll figure out something."

I sank into him, knowing that nothing was going to fix this. He knew it too. He'd said the words, but we both knew I'd crossed a line I couldn't come back from.

Chapter Twenty-Nine

IT TOOK us two days to get back. The bike we'd found died at the base of the mountain road that led to the pack. We walked back into the Arkansas pack on foot. probably looking like we'd just escaped with our lives. We had. We'd changed our clothes, cleaned off in a river, but nothing about us looked the same. I definitely wasn't the same, and the closer you looked, the more you could feel it. I could feel the change pulsing through me, changing me.

But something about the changes had been freeing. All my confusion—the debate on what to do, where to go—had disappeared. This was Kicks' home. If I left, so would he. I wasn't doing that to him, and screw anyone who thought I should. I didn't care what the pack thought of me anymore. The only thing that mattered was Kicks. This was where he needed to be. The people here loved him, and he loved them. And it wasn't just Kicks. Charlie would have a good life here if Kicks was the alpha, even if I became something beyond recognition. They deserved to have this place.

As we walked into the community, people came out of

their homes and buildings. There was a mixture of expressions upon their faces, from smiles, as they saw Kicks, to fear, as they saw me. Some rushed forward. Some hung back, skeptical because I was beside him.

Evangeline rushed over to us, giving Kicks a fierce hug.

"How are you two?" she said.

"We're good," Kicks said.

"We heard some crazy stories," Crackers said, joining us.

"They're probably all true," I said.

"Wow, badass." Crackers nodded.

Kicks glanced at me. I'd given him the broad strokes on the trip home. I had a feeling he'd be getting a more embellished version soon.

Death had wanted the story to spread, and it looked like it was moving faster than the plague in the Middle Ages.

"You want to go get washed up?" Kicks asked, giving me an out to go tuck myself away in the cabin.

"No. I need to say something first, and I want to do it now."

He knew that the *last* thing I'd ever wanted to do in the past was address the pack. "Should we talk about this first?"

"No." It wouldn't change anything, so I was doing this now.

Both of us were dead on our feet, but I felt surer of this than anything I'd done in a year. I walked over to one of the picnic tables and called out, "I need your attention."

It didn't take long to get it, since most of them hadn't stopped staring at us since we walked in. Still, I waited until every last set of eyes were focused on me because I was only going to say this once. If they didn't hear it, that was their problem.

"I'm sure all of you here want to know what's going on,

256

where we've been. Some of you have probably already heard some gossip."

I was pretty sure anyone with a satellite phone had called everyone they could after the bloodbath at Dirkin's. From some of the evasive looks, it was clear they'd heard.

"This is Kicks' home. He grew up here. You're his pack, and that runs deep for an alpha, especially one such as him. He didn't want to leave here, ever, and I know you didn't want him to go. The same can't be said for me. At least some of you want me gone." There were no denials from the hushed crowd. "Well, I've got bad news for you, because I'm not going anywhere. If this is where Kicks wants to be, I'll be staying as well."

I let that sink in, waiting to see if there was a revolt. When the crowd didn't seem to go wild, I continued. "If your intentions toward me and my family are pure, we won't have a problem. If you're okay with humans, that bodes well for you. If you *don't* like me or Charlie, if you don't like humans, come and find me. It'll be easy, because I won't be hiding. Odds are, you won't live long enough to cause me a problem. On the other end of the spectrum, if your intent is good, we'll be fine. Just know this place is going to be my son's home and I will protect it with my life."

The crowd looked stunned. I could see Evangeline and Crackers in the back, looking at each other and then nodding, as if they could live with my terms.

I'd turned to climb off the table when a lone voice in the crowd called, "Wait."

I turned out of curiosity. It didn't matter what they wanted or what they thought of me anymore. I'd made my choices, and I was good with them.

A girl stepped forward. I'd seen her before, but she'd

never spoken to me, always seeming to leave a buffer between us.

I waited for her to speak, not bothering to soften my expression. I no longer cared enough.

"Is it true that they poisoned Kicks? That they threw him in a hole to die?" Her eyes were large, as if she couldn't believe what she'd heard.

"Yes. That's exactly what *shifters* did to him." They might not have been of the same pack, but they were shifters. They weren't *other*, like me. For so long I'd been treated as less than because they could shift. Well, there was her kind in action. Let her claim them.

"And you saved him?" she said, not reacting or smarting from the barb I'd thrown her way.

I scanned the rest of the crowd, and no one seemed insulted by my words, at least not outwardly.

"Yes. In a manner of speaking, I did." It felt strange to claim that deed when it had truly been Death's doing, but try explaining that to this crowd. It was easier to just own it. And after all, I'd be paying the price for it. Why shouldn't I take credit?

An older woman, one I remembered for her sharp looks, stepped forward. This was probably where the witch hunt would start. It would end quickly, because I wasn't going anywhere, not right away, not until it was time, and good luck to anyone who thought they could make me.

"There's a rumor that some among our kind had a hand in Death Day. Is that true?" Her voice held a wobble, as if the truth truly rattled her to her core.

It didn't make me soften to her at all.

"If by 'a hand,' you mean 'orchestrated the death of most of *my* kind'? Then yes. That's true as well." I had a lot more to add on that if she pushed the subject. Her kind, which she'd thought so superior, had nearly wiped out my race and then looked down upon me. At this point, I was hoping she'd give me an excuse to lay into her further.

She didn't. She dropped her head, nodding and then mumbling something.

"What did you say?" I asked.

Kicks, who'd been standing silently beside the table, reached over and grabbed my hand. "She apologized," he said.

I'd heard him clearly but didn't believe the words he'd said. "What?"

"I'm sorry," the woman said loudly.

I turned to see her looking at me with an open expression that looked genuine.

Now *I* was speechless.

"I judged you as unworthy," she said. "I thought you were a plague on our pack, and I was wrong. You were purging the evil from our ranks, strengthening us."

I still couldn't seem to find my words as Kicks squeezed my hand. I ran my eyes over the rest of the pack. As if they understood my shock, several of them nodded, and there were murmurs of thanks through the group.

"Thank you for returning to us," another woman said.

There were nods and more murmurs of thanks.

I nodded back, still dumbfounded. I hadn't known what to expect, but this wasn't it.

I turned, and Kicks lifted me off the table. He took my hand, leading me toward the cabin.

He shut the door and then leaned against it, staring at me.

"Did you mean all that?" he asked.

"Every word. This is your home, and I don't want you to lose that." If I still had one, I'd be holding on for dear life.

"Every time I think I can't be more amazed by you, I am."

He stared at me as if I were truly something phenomenal. I dropped my gaze to the floor.

"What?" he said. "You just stared down a pack you used to be afraid to walk among, but you can't face a couple compliments?"

"I'm not amazing. I'm just doing what has to be done," I said.

I didn't want to be cold to him. I had to be. We both knew what was coming, and his joking wouldn't make it easier in the end.

"If you don't mind, I could use a few minutes," I said, walking toward the bedroom.

He stayed there, leaning against the door, his disappointment so thick it nearly broke me. As brave as he thought I was, I rushed to the bedroom and shut the door so I didn't break in front of him.

Chapter Thirty

THE PACK STARED at me as I walked to the river, one of my favorite spots to relax. We'd been back a month, but the weather was still frigid. It didn't bother me as I took off my boots and dipped my feet in the water. I'd listen to the birds sing while the pack stared and whispered.

Things were different now. Gone were the days I'd hide. The day after we returned, there was an exodus of about ten percent of the pack. My speech had hit home, and the members who disliked me fled. The ones left probably didn't hold any ill will toward me, but they kept their distance. I was like a god among them that they didn't quite know how to approach. I was okay with that.

They gave me my space, and I didn't encourage them to come any closer, not while I still didn't know what I'd become. There was no sense in forming more relationships with these people when I didn't know how long I'd be here. Even Evangeline and Buddie seemed hesitant, as if waiting for some cue from me on how to proceed. I couldn't give them something when I didn't know myself. Rastin still insisted on seeking me out whenever he could, as if bludgeoning me with his talks would somehow make me go back to normal.

Charlie waved to me from where he was playing with the kids. I waved back. He could sense the change in me too, although he seemed more willing to accept it.

Just last week he'd asked, "Why do you seem different?"

I'd told him, "I'm becoming tougher so that no one will ever run us out of our home again."

"When I can shift into a monster, I'll help you," he'd said. Then he'd smiled and gone back to playing.

He would, too, not that he was going to need to. No one would ever mess with him while I was alive.

I spotted Kicks heading toward me. No matter where I went in the afternoon, he seemed to seek me out. Maybe it was because he was no longer sleeping at the cabin, by my request. Either way, he'd come. Sometimes he'd sit silently and sometimes he'd force a conversation. It was a coin toss which I was getting today.

He settled in, close but not touching.

"You're going to get past this."

Just great. It was going to be a conversation day.

"I'm not getting past anything," I said. "I've realized what I'm willing to do to protect the people around me and accepted it. I made a deal. I'm not the person I was, and I'm okay with it, even if you aren't." The bottom line was that I'd have to be okay with it, because there was no backing out once I made a deal with Death.

"*This* isn't who you are."

"I don't think you realize who I am anymore. I'm not only accepting the change, I'm happy for it. You might not be, but I am. I'm okay with being the monster people fear if that's what this world requires." At least I'd be able to protect them, if nothing else.

"You'll never be a monster."

He said that now, but he didn't know what was coming, what Death would turn me into. I'd come to terms with it and would deal with what came. After what they'd done to Kicks, after they'd killed so many people the way they had, they all deserved it. I knew what Death needed me to be, and I wasn't delusional about the price that would be paid. He'd see me for what I was becoming eventually and stop trying to force the issue. I had to be ready for that. We all needed to be ready to accept I might not be *me* soon.

"Why would you come back if you were intent on living like this?" he asked. There was such sadness in his tone that the part of me still untouched wanted to reach out and comfort him. I would've if it wouldn't only prolong the hurt.

Instead I said, "It was the best option." I didn't add that it was for them. No one would touch them or their home, and being here was the best way to make sure of that, at least while I could.

His gaze was off in the distance, and I could tell my words, as practical and cold as ever, had cut him. That was okay. It was good, even. It might burn right now, but it would help him move on from me. I wouldn't be the woman for him after *she* was through with me. I wouldn't be the woman for anyone after this was all done.

"I know what you're doing, and it's not going to work," he said. "I won't give up on you. I know what you've been through, how helpless you've felt and how terrifying it was, but don't shut down every feeling. That's too high a price."

Hope flared in my chest, but I stomped it out quickly. If somehow I made it out of this retaining some of my humanity, then just maybe we could have a future. Right now, that seemed like a slim possibility. I could already feel the person I'd been getting pulled into the darkness growing inside.

"The price has already been agreed to. It's done and I'm not sorry for it. You need to let it go." My voice was steadier than I'd imagined I could make it.

"No." The word hit like a clap of thunder.

"Why?" I said, afraid he'd heard the crack in my voice with that one word.

"Because I can't." He tensed, looking like he wasn't even breathing anymore. He just stood there, the intensity nearly making me want to buckle and agree with him.

The darkness inside me pulsed strong, trying to lure me with the comfort of numbness, to pull me away from the emotions that made me human. It would be so easy to let it take control, obliterate all this panic and fear running through me.

"I know it's not what you wanted," I said. "Still, you need to accept what lies ahead. I'll never be the person you need me to be, not now." He deserved someone whole, not me the way I was now, or what I'd become.

I could feel the tension pouring off him. "You are the only person I want, and if you think I'm going to give up, you don't know me."

He locked eyes with me, as if forcing me to accept his will. It took another moment before he turned and walked away.

It changed nothing. I'd done what I'd done and I didn't regret it. I'd live with the repercussions. He'd be alive and safe. Death would protect him, and I clung to that as I watched him retreat.

The darkness surged inside me, offering to obliterate the

pain, but I pushed it back. If I could just make it through what came next, maybe, just maybe…

Death appeared beside me, watching Kicks' retreat.

Don't even look at him. He's off-limits, and so is anyone else in this pack unless I say otherwise.

"Who are you to give me orders?" she said.

I'm the only one who's going to reap your revenge, that's who.

She watched me, tilting her head to one side and then the other. "You're changing, human. Or should I even call you that anymore?"

Maybe I am.

"I *like* it."

At least one of us did.

Everything was going to change. Things had already shifted in me. I could feel it, and Kicks could too. I'd gambled my future to secure his and Charlie's, and it was a bargain I'd keep. Any hope I'd had for a happily ever after was dangling by the thinnest thread.

Look for book four of Life After Death Day later this year.

Can't wait that long for more post-apocalyptic shifter fantasy from Donna Augustine? Read the completed series The Wilds now.

scan the QR code to join my mailing list.

FOLLOW ME ON ONE OF THESE PLATFORMS:
https://www.facebook.com/groups/223180598486878/
http://www.donnaaugustine.com
https://www.bookbub.com/authors/donna-augustine
https://twitter.com/DonnAugustine

Acknowledgments

Donna Z., I've had to publish without you on occasion but boy do I hate it! I'm so happy you're back and better than ever!

Lori K., your contribution truly made this a better book!

Lisa A., always relieved when I get your stamp of approval and insight on a story!

Camilla J., I always know if you say it's good to go, it's really good to go. Your honesty is treasure!

Karen C., you had some really good catches this go around!! You'll never know how relieved I am that you caught them!

That was a lot of exclamations, but it had to be done.

Also by Donna Augustine

The Wilds (Post-apocalyptic)

The Wilds

The Hunt

The Dead

The Magic

Born Wild (Wilds Spinoff)

Wild One

Savage One

Wyrd Blood (Post-apocalyptic)

Wyrd Blood

Full Blood

Blood Binds

Ollie Wit

A Step into the Dark

Walking in the Dark

Kissed by the Dark

Going Nowhere

A Bridge to Nowhereland

Burning Bridges in Nowhere

Out of Nowhere

The Keepers

The Keepers

Keepers and Killers

Shattered

Redemption

Karma

Karma

Jinxed

Fated

Dead Ink

Torn Worlds (Paranormal Romance)

Gut Deep

Visceral Reaction

River of Luck

Tales of Xest

The Whimsy Witch Who Wasn't

The Nowhere Witch

The Most Wanted Witch

Witch of all Witches